# ASSIGNED A DADDY

### EMILY TILTON

# CHAPTER ONE

Darla got the terrible email on Friday, March 3, 2067.

*Dear Miss Hawkins:*

*Pursuant to statute 57(a)(i)(c) of the Uniform Penal Act of 2045, your correctional action for the misdemeanor to which you pled guilty in absentia 15 February 2067 has been contracted to Selecta Corporation. After an extensive review by our Pertailored™ team, we have determined that your psychological profile presents a perfect fit for our 'Daddy's Naughty Little Girl' unit. Your daddy will arrive at your home the morning of Sunday, March 5, to take you into custody and bring you home with him, where you will spend at least the next six months.*

*We advise you to consult our website, selectacorrection.com/daddy as soon as possible for information on what to expect and how to prepare.*

*Sincerely,*
*Otto Herndon*
*Corrections Analyst*
*Selecta Corporation*

The email itself wasn't nearly as terrible, though, as what Darla found when she clicked on the link.

*Hi! You're probably reading this page because you'll soon be getting a visit from a Selecta correctional officer who will take you into custody and serve as your daddy. We want you to understand your correction as fully as you can before it happens. You're probably going to be quite nervous, especially if this is your first offense.*

Well, it certainly wasn't Darla's first offense, but her two prior ones, both for shoplifting—like this one—had been handled by Homenture Corporation. She remembered now seeing an item in a news crawl about the contract being taken away from Homenture. She had paid no attention, of course, because none of that stuff made any difference: the next time she got caught, she would spend more time picking up trash at the mall, whether the guards' uniforms said *Homenture* or *Selecta.*

But, yes, she felt so nervous she was nearly hyperventilating. 'Daddy's Naughty Little Girl'? What the fuck did that mean?

*Go ahead and watch this video. As embarrassing as you may find it, we think you'll realize that our Pertailored™ approach has identified you correctly as needing exactly this kind of correction. Pertailored™ is based on a robust, proprietary dataset that none of our competition can match, and so we have no doubt at all that it's the right program for you.*

Heart beating wildly in her chest, Darla clicked on the video's play button. The blue corporate logo of Selecta—the 'a' had a smiley face—gave way to a pink title: 'Daddy's Naughty Little Girl: a program for nonviolent offenders.' Accompanying the title, over a black screen, was a cartoon of a girl with blue eyes and blond pigtails, though she was clearly an adult. The girl turned her head over her shoulder to look at the viewer with a sorrowful expression on her face.

The girl wore nothing but a cloth diaper, and she had

put her hand down to her left bottom-cheek, covered in that thick fabric, as if… as if the diaper covered a backside that someone had just spanked.

Darla felt a blush building in her cheeks and rapidly claiming her whole face.

The title faded, and a shot came up of a little girl's room, complete with pink frills on the pillow shams. A man's voice, deep and a little stern, said, "We know you want to be a good girl, sweetheart. We know you want to obey the law and have a happy life. Things went wrong in your life, but we're going to take you back to that place where you felt safe and loved. You've been naughty, but from now on you're going to be daddy's good little girl."

A girl with light brown hair, about twenty, came into the room and went to sit on the bed. She wore something very old-fashioned—was it a pinafore, Darla wondered? Is that what that apron-y thing was called? Darla felt her blush grow hotter as she speculated on whether the girl wore a diaper underneath.

A man entered—tall, blond, quite handsome. He wore a nice Oxford shirt and wool slacks, just what Darla's own father had used to wear to work. He stood in front of the girl, who looked down at her hands in her lap. He spoke, in a voice different from that of the voiceover narration but, like that other voice, very authoritative.

"You know what I have to do, Francie, don't you?" he asked.

"Yes, daddy," the girl said.

Just the words. Just *Yes, daddy* sent a jolt of shame and fear up Darla's spine as she watched. She tried desperately not to put herself in Francie's place in her imagination, but utterly failed.

"You left the house without permission, didn't you?" The man's voice had become very stern.

Francie looked up with fear in her eyes. "I'm sorry, daddy! Please, not on the bare!"

*Oh, no*, Darla thought. *Please, no.*

"Of course on the bare, honey. You know I have to. This is the second rule you've broken this week. I spanked you over your drawers on Monday, but it seems like that didn't work. Take off everything, right now. You're going to have a special lesson."

"No!" Francie wailed. "It's so… please don't, daddy. Just a spanking, please?"

"You know as well as I do, Francie, that sometimes only a special lesson will teach you how to behave. Get your dress and underwear off right now, or I'm going to have to use my belt."

Darla's gasp burst from her throat. This couldn't be real. It couldn't happen to her.

"Not the belt, daddy!" Francie cried. "It hurts so much!"

"Then do as I say, honey, and get ready for your special lesson. Naked on the bed, with your bottom up. I'm going to go get the trainer ready."

The scene froze, with Francie starting to take off her pinafore and her daddy turning away. Darla felt like her curiosity might actually kill her at that moment. What would happen to Francie? What was a *special lesson*? What kind of a *trainer* did her daddy mean? Surely not a person—but then, what? She had to almost physically stop herself from trying to puzzle it out, because too many terrible visions began to fill her mind. She took her right wrist in her left hand, nearly unconsciously, and held it fast.

The voiceover returned. "Sweetheart, Selecta does its homework very thoroughly. We know you need exactly what you just saw Francie about to get: her daddy's firm hand, guiding her and, when necessary, correcting her. Your own daddy will come to get you, very soon now. Here's what you have to do to get ready."

The screen faded back to black, and as the voiceover continued, the words appeared there, as bullet points.

"First, make sure to pack clothes and other necessities

4

for a week's stay. Your daddy will have other clothes for you, too, but if you behave yourself you'll be allowed to wear your own clothes much of the time. Second, collect your vital papers and bills. You'll be staying with your daddy for at least six months. He will drive you to your workplace, pick you up, and supervise your day-to-day affairs. Third and finally, prepare yourself to obey your daddy. He is permitted by law to punish you as he sees fit, as long as he does not injure you, and to stimulate you sexually by any means he chooses, though he may not have non-consensual sex with you."

*Special lesson.* Oh, God…

The bullet points remained, as the voiceover said, "We feel sure, sweetheart, that someday soon you'll feel so grateful to your daddy, and to the Selecta Corporation, that you won't even remember how nervous you are right now. Your daddy will make those butterflies in your tummy fly away, and leave a good little girl behind."

•  •  •  •  •  •  •

When the doorbell of her apartment buzzed at nine a.m. on Sunday, Darla, though still in a state of shock over what she had seen in the video, had all her things packed in two suitcases that waited by the door. She pushed the intercom button and said, in a voice that sounded quavery to her own ears, "Hi, I'll be right down."

But a voice even deeper than the video voiceovers said, "Stay there, Darla. Buzz me in, please."

"No," Darla said desperately into the intercom. "I'll come down. I'm all ready. You can start your… your daddy business… stuff… when we get to your house, okay?"

"No, I won't," said the voice of the man whom Darla realized she had immediately begun to think of as her daddy. "We have some things to go over before I take you home to my house. We've already started your correctional

program. And by disobeying me you just earned yourself your first spanking. Buzz me in."

Darla stepped back from the intercom, breathing in ragged pants. She watched her left hand move to the orange button that would unlock the apartment lobby to her daddy. She watched her finger push the button. She heard the distant sound of the buzzer, and the opening and closing of the big door one flight down.

She had the wild thought of calling the police, but she saw in her mind's eye exactly what would happen. This man—her daddy—would show a badge and a contract, and then he would… spank her even harder. Maybe he would even ask the policemen if they wanted to watch him spank Darla.

A sharp knock on the door. Darla felt like running away, trying to hide in the closet.

"Darla, sweetheart," the man's voice said. "Don't make this worse, please. You know what I can do. You watched the video. I know you did, because when you clicked play it registered in your file. I'm allowed to break down the door if I have to, but I don't want you to have to pay for that."

Darla reached out to the doorknob, hardly believing she could turn it, then hardly believing she *was* turning it. She pulled, and the door opened to reveal a tall, tall man with a broad chest and a chiseled chin. He had short, dark brown hair, and chocolate brown eyes. He wore a black T-shirt and crisp jeans—with a wide, brown leather belt that had a star on its buckle. Something about him screamed *military* so loudly that Darla found herself taking a step backward.

He smiled, but did not move forward. He had a pink garment bag over his shoulder, Darla noticed now, and a shopping bag in his left hand.

"Hello, Darla," he said. "I'm Mike Beckwith. I'm going to be your daddy for the next six months at least."

"Hi," Darla said, very uncertainly.

"Hi, *daddy*," Mike corrected. "You have to call me daddy whenever you speak. It helps you remember that you're my little girl."

Darla's jaw hung slack, then she closed her mouth and swallowed hard. She couldn't seem to get enough saliva to speak.

"That's okay, sweetheart," Mike said. "I'm a very patient daddy, I think you'll find. Say *Hi, daddy* whenever you're ready."

"Hi, daddy," Darla finally managed to squeak.

"There," Mike said. "Perfect. Good girl."

*Oh, no.* Those words. *Good girl.*

"Now let's go into your living room, Darla. There are some things we have to discuss, and you're going to have to change your clothes. Then you'll have your spanking."

"What?" Darla asked, aghast. "The video said… I mean it said I'd be able to wear my own clothes."

"When I allow it," Mike said, dropping his chin a little and looking at her through narrowed eyes. "I'm not going to allow it today. Today you'll wear your pinafore, and if you're a good girl for me you'll wear your own clothes to work in the morning."

Again Darla's jaw dropped. Surely there was no possibility she would have to wear *to work* that thing Francie in the video had worn?

"Like I said, sweetheart, I'm a patient man. But when a girl doesn't do as she's told, I give her the guidance she's looking for. I don't want to have to make your first spanking harder for you than it needs to be, but I'm starting to think it needs to be more of a real lesson than I'd supposed. Are you going to go to the living room or not?"

"Yes," Darla whispered.

"Yes, what?"

"Yes, daddy."

# CHAPTER TWO

Mike followed petite, brunette Darla to the tiny living room of her apartment, already feeling a little bewitched by her dark eyes. Yes, this assignment would be just as enjoyable as his new boss Otto had told him.

"It'll be very different from what you're used to, colonel."

"Please," Mike had said. "Not a colonel anymore, thank goodness. Different is good."

"You weren't happy in the military?" Otto's brow creased, on the other side of the walnut desk in this thirty-sixth floor corner office of the Selecta building in Los Angeles.

"Oh, I liked the military fine, and I'm going to miss my men. But it's not the kind of life I wanted to get older in."

Otto nodded sagely. "Exactly. I think you're going to have a fine career here at Selecta. Your profile says you're a perfect fit for our DNLG program—that's *Daddy's Naughty Little Girl*."

For a moment, Mike hadn't thought he had heard correctly, and it must have shown on his face because Otto chuckled.

"It's our new program. Synergized with our more

standard programs, some of which employ corporal punishment and some of which are just supervised community service and the like. The outcomes are through the roof."

Mike felt his eyebrows go up. "Okay, tell me more."

"Selecta was founded as a corporate offshoot of something that you might as well think of as an LLC, called the Institute. The Institute has a lot of experience with analyzing and modifying female behavior in the erotic realm. You may or may not know that there's a certain subset of women who respond well, behaviorally speaking, to being *regressed*, as it's usually called." Otto pushed a folder across the desk. "Darla here is a very good example, though she doesn't know it as far as we can tell. May have had some fantasies, but probably repressed them."

"Regressed?"

"Your job, should you choose to accept it, will be to make Darla feel like a little girl again, so that she can rethink her conduct and set out on a new adult path—a much more constructive one. You'll discipline her the old-fashioned way, but you'll also incorporate certain things we call *big-girl* training activities that bring her sexuality into the scope of her correctional program."

"Ah," Mike had said. He had seen where Otto was going now. "Yes, I think that program will be a good fit for me."

Now he watched Darla look around her living room uncertainly, carefully planning his next move.

"Stand in front of the couch, sweetheart," he said. She looked back at him with startled eyes and obeyed. Mike sat and reached out his hands. Darla shied back.

"Give me your hands, Darla," he said patiently, not yet injecting any sternness into his voice.

"Why?" He heard the quaver in her voice, and his heart went out to her, but he knew he had to start correctly.

"Why, *what*?"

"Why, daddy?" The quaver had become real fear.

"Because I said so, sweetheart. Give me your hands, or you'll feel my belt across your naughty rump in a few minutes instead of just my hand."

"Oh, God," Darla whispered, but she stepped forward and held out her hands for Mike to grasp them gently in his own. She started at his touch, but didn't pull her hands away.

"Look at how small your hands are in mine," he said softly.

She did look. "Yes, daddy," she said in the same whisper, almost as if he had hypnotized her.

"I'm Mike Beckwith. I used to be in the marines, but now I work for Selecta, and I'll be your daddy."

Darla looked up quickly, and then back down at their hands as if concerned that she might not be allowed to look at Mike.

"You can go ahead and look at me, Darla," Mike said gently. "It's alright."

She raised her eyes to his again, and he smiled at her. Her chin quivered. "Please don't spank me, daddy," she said.

Mike sighed. "I have to, sweetheart. You have a lot to learn, and it all begins right here. You've had no consistency in your life, let alone any discipline. If I didn't make you sorry that you disobeyed me, especially when I've promised you a spanking, I would start your program off completely wrong, wouldn't I?"

Darla looked down, and a tear splashed onto Mike's right hand.

"Wouldn't I, Darla?"

"Y-yes, daddy," she breathed.

"Alright. Your daddy isn't a man who does a lot of pondering, but the nice thing about the program they've put you in is that neither of us has to think about it very much. I know how to be a daddy and you know how to be a little girl. So get those grownup clothes off, and put on your pinafore and your little-girl underwear." Mike

released her hands.

"Okay, daddy," Darla said, seeming to resolve at least to try to be a good girl. She picked up the garment bag and the shopping bag and headed for the bedroom. "I'll be right out."

Mike shook his head. "No, you won't. You'll get undressed right here, and then dressed again."

"What?" Darla said. "You're kidding me. I mean, you're kidding me, daddy. Right?"

"No, sweetheart. That's another thing you have to start getting used to right away. You lost the right to privacy when you got convicted of your third misdemeanor. Your daddy gets to inspect you naked, and decide on your grooming and hygiene. You'll be inspected every day, to make sure you're taking good care of yourself. Also, daddy will decide if it's time for big-girl training, or special lessons, which involve your pussy and your anus."

"H-how do I make sure… I mean, daddy… How d-do I…" The bags shook in Darla's hands.

"How do you avoid big-girl training and special lessons?" Mike asked. "You don't sweetheart. They're part of being daddy's naughty little girl."

"T-today, daddy?"

Mike smiled. "No, Darla. Not today. I promise I'll get you nice and ready, and you'll have several inspections before your first big-girl training."

He saw the gratitude break out on Darla's face, which made him very happy.

"Now get those jeans off, sweetheart. It's time we got started."

She started to turn around, but Mike said, "No, Darla, I want to see everything. Put the bags right down and get undressed."

Her mouth set itself into a tight line, and she looked down at the floor. Mike reached out and gently took the bags from her. Darla looked up and he could tell that she saw in his eyes the sympathy he felt, because her face took

on a thoughtful expression, as if she were having trouble figuring something out.

"I know this is hard," Mike said. "But you know you've been a very naughty girl, don't you? Stealing all that stuff?"

Darla nodded. Mike waited. Darla whispered, "Yes, daddy. I… I needed it, or I thought I did, but…"

"But what, sweetheart?"

"But that's no excuse." She looked down at the dark green pile carpet again.

"Can you see why you have to make a big change in your life?"

"Yes, but… I mean, yes, daddy… b-but…" A tear rolled down her cheek.

"You're scared?" She nodded, but he let it go without demanding that she speak. "Of being spanked like a naughty little girl?"

"And… the other things." Her eyes darted up nervously to meet his, and then back down. He could see now that she had started to tremble. Mike put the bags on the couch next to him and opened his arms.

"I'm going to hug you now, Darla," he said. "Little girls don't just get spankings and inspections from their daddies—they get big hugs and cuddles, too."

She looked up into his eyes, her brow furrowed in confusion, as if she hadn't considered this dimension at all. "But… I thought… I mean, it's supposed to be a punishment, isn't it? Having a daddy and going to live with you… daddy?"

Darla looked like she wanted to come into Mike's arms, but also like she thought it might be a trick. The hesitant expression on her pretty face tugged at his heartstrings, and he wondered for a moment whether something more might come of this assignment than just six months of supervising a wayward girl for Selecta. Corporate correctional officers were explicitly allowed to form romantic attachments with custodial offenders, provided the relationship could be verified as consensual by a

certified third party.

"It's a correction, sweetheart. Sometimes correction involves punishment, and I'm afraid that it definitely will involve punishment for you, because we both know it's going to take a while for you to become the good girl we both want you to be. It'll certainly involve a spanking for you in just a little while, and even before that it'll involve you taking off all your clothes for me right now. But it has to involve rewards and encouragements, too, or it just won't work. So come here, please, and let me hug you."

Darla's little mouth twitched as if she were going to say something in question or protest, but she took two little steps forward and let him put his arms around her. She trembled for a moment in his arms and resisted the embrace, but suddenly, with a little sob, she seemed to melt into Mike's chest and clung to him. He snuggled her face into his shirt as she sniffled, and he rubbed her back through the concert T-shirt of a boy band that had broken up five years before.

"You haven't had much cuddling, sweetheart, have you?" Mike said quietly.

She shook her head, her chin moving gently against Mike's pectoral muscles. "No, daddy," she said. "Never."

"Well, we're going to fix that."

"Okay, daddy."

He held her a minute longer, feeling the tension go out of her, and then he said. "Do you think you're ready to get changed, now?"

"Oh," Darla said, as if she had forgotten all about that—or, more probably, had hoped he had forgotten about it. "Do I really, really have to, daddy?"

Mike smiled, because he heard in her voice that she had begun to fall into the beginnings of her regression.

"Yes, sweetheart, you really, really have to." He reached down and rubbed her bottom, a little distracted by its rather extraordinary pertness in the skinny jeans, and gave it a little squeeze that made Darla jump. "There's a bottom

here that needs warming."

He released her from the hug, and she stepped back, looking down again, shamefaced and blushing. She compressed her lips into a tight line, deepened the furrow on her brow, and started to take off her T-shirt.

Mike watched in silence, wishing he could tell his cock not to get hard at the sight of pretty little Darla taking off her adult clothes to change into her pinafore, so that she could have her first spanking from her daddy. But, as he'd read in the training manual, it went with the job: girls like Darla needed big doses of nudity in front of their daddies to feel the proper shame and modesty.

She put the T-shirt on the coffee table.

"You don't wear a bra, sweetheart?" Her perfect little breasts were even more pert than her bottom, if that was possible, with sweet brown nipples just about the size of a quarter.

She looked at him bashfully. "No, daddy. My breasts are so small I don't need one." She hesitated, as if trying to decide whether to say something. Then she said, in an even more little-girlish tone, "Do I?"

"No, sweetheart, you don't. And you certainly won't wear one with your pinafore. Go ahead and take your jeans off, now. Leave your panties on for a moment so daddy can see what kind of panties you wear."

Darla chewed the inside of her cheek for a moment. "I'm not wearing panties, daddy," she confessed.

"Darla!" Mike said, genuinely—if slightly—shocked. "Don't you know better than that? Little girls who don't wear their panties need to learn some important lessons about taking care of their bodies."

"I packed all the clean ones in my bag before I got dressed, and I didn't want to take any of them out." Her mouth twisted adorably to the side.

"Well, since you weren't in my custody when you got dressed, I can't spank you for it—plus you've got one coming anyway for the disobedience—but we'll discuss

this at tomorrow's inspection. I can promise you that if you go without your underwear while you're with me, whether you're wearing grownup clothes or little-girl clothes, you'll have trouble sitting down for a day or two."

"What about at night?" she asked, obviously curious all of a sudden.

"No panties under your nighty, of course," Mike said. "But I need to tell you right away that I believe naughty little girls shouldn't touch their pussies unless their daddies give them permission, as a reward for good behavior."

# CHAPTER THREE

He couldn't be serious, could he? Darla felt her jaw drop.

"Do you play with yourself often, sweetheart?" Mike asked. How could he make such a horrible question sound so reasonable, as if he really did have the right, as Darla's daddy, to ask it?

She stared at him, willing him to laugh and make it clear that he had tried to make a terrible joke. He looked back at her gravely. "I can understand you not wanting to answer me, Darla, but you need to get this clear in your mind right now: when your daddy asks you a question, you answer it, no matter how embarrassing, or you get punished. Do you understand?"

Darla realized her breath had once again begun to come in short, ragged pants. Every time he said *punished* her whole body seemed to flash hot—everywhere, unfortunately. Somehow the Selecta people had known. Something about her seemed to say that what Mike was doing was not only acceptable but… necessary.

"Yes, daddy," she whispered. She looked down at the carpet. Green pile. She hated that carpet. She hated this apartment, whose rent had encouraged her to shoplift

three times, just to have clothes that made her feel like she could hold her head up at work.

"Now answer my question, sweetheart. Do you play with your little pussy, to make yourself feel good?"

"S-sometimes," Darla stammered.

"Thank you for being honest, Darla," Mike replied, nodding in approval and once again presenting Darla with the problem of her apparent *need*—ten minutes after meeting her 'daddy'—for that approval. "Most nights I'll give you permission to touch yourself, if you've obeyed me and respected me that day. You won't have permission to do it anywhere but in bed, though, after dark. If I catch you with your hand there, when you don't have permission, you'll have a bare-bottom belt-whipping."

*Oh, God.* Darla felt her face burning like the sun. Yes, she masturbated sometimes... but when times got a little rough, *often* probably made a better representation of it. At least she'd be able to touch herself in the bathroom.

"And don't think you'll be able to do it in the bathroom either, in my house, because you're going to be doing your business with the door open, so I can see you, and I'm going to supervise your bathing. At work, you're going to text me for permission to go to the bathroom, and then put your phone where you can record yourself peeing so I can watch it later."

Darla started to shake her head. It couldn't be real, could it? And yet... and yet it was, and her mind didn't reel the way she thought it should. Her face kept right on blazing, but Mike's paternal authority, even in this extraordinarily shameful area, seemed to embrace her. His tone, and the detail with which he had thought out the implementation of Darla's correctional program, told her that the purpose of the program had to lie much more in her reform than in her humiliation.

That didn't mean Darla had to like it, though. She had to push back, even if it got her a worse punishment now.

"That's mean, daddy," she said, realizing to her surprise

that she had begun to take on the persona of a little girl without even thinking about it. "I won't do that. It's not fair, and it's creepy and shameful."

She looked up at Mike in apprehension, and saw to her shock that his face had utterly transformed itself into an expression of restrained anger, his eyebrows lowered and his mouth set. He didn't speak, at first, but he reached out and took Darla by her hips and pulled her a step toward him, as her arms spun around in the air, seeking her balance.

She needn't have worried about that, because Mike had such strength even just in his hands that there was no chance Darla might fall. He had his hands in the waistband of her jeans, now, and before she knew it he had them unbuttoned and he was pulling them down. Darla gave a little cry of surprise and humiliation to know that her daddy now saw her pussy, with its sparse brown thatch, for the first time.

Mike spoke again at last. "You just earned yourself quite the spanking, sweetheart, and in the nude. Your new little-girl panties are going to feel pretty sore on your little bottom in a few minutes."

"Please, no… please, daddy…" Darla wailed. But she understood too late that although Mike certainly had told the truth when he said he was a patient man, she had pushed him much too far, since he also clearly felt keenly his responsibility to start setting boundaries for Darla. He didn't speak again, but pulled her between his thighs and bent her over his left knee.

Wild now to escape the spanking somehow, anyhow, Darla threw her right hand back and put it across her tender bottom cheeks. But Mike grabbed her wrist in his right hand and transferred it to his left so that he could pin it with terrible ease against the small of her back. At the same time, he closed his thighs around hers, immobilizing her almost completely.

"You'll learn to hold still for your punishments," Mike

said, that same controlled anger in his voice. "It starts with knowing that you don't have a choice, when your daddy decides your butt needs whipping."

The words frightened Darla so much that she tried to writhe away even though her mind told her Mike spoke the truth when he said it wouldn't help. With every ounce of her strength, and probably extra from the fear, she struggled against him, but she couldn't manage to slip from his grasp more than an inch. Her naked bottom, ready for his discipline, still rose over his thigh.

He put his hand on it, and Darla used her millimeter of freedom to flinch, although the touch was gentle.

"This is a very special moment for you, Darla," Mike said much more softly than she would have expected. "I know you're scared, and you should be, because I'm going to teach you the first real lesson of your life, but I promise you're going to look back on this spanking with gratitude. You earned a bare-bottom punishment, and you're about to get it, just as you'll probably get many more, before being a good girl becomes second nature to you. While I give you what you've got coming, I want you to think about what it means, to have your daddy take down your jeans and tan your hide because you couldn't obey him, and then you disrespected him. Do you think you can do that?"

"Yes, d-daddy," Darla whimpered, as Mike kept rubbing her bottom. It felt like worse torture than the spanking ever could be, because it felt so good, and his words were so soothing.

But the hand left off rubbing, and she knew he had begun to wind up his arm. Then a little puff of air. Then the sharp slap, and the pain, in the very middle of her bottom. Darla yelped, squirmed. But another spank landed, on her right cheek, and then another on her left, and her yelps had become cries of pain, because Mike was spanking very hard indeed, moving at a never-varying pace from center to right to left, as if thoroughly painting

Darla's bottom with fire. After a minute of the spanking, she felt her bottom starting to squirm on its own, as if desperate to assuage the pain, clenching and unclenching under her daddy's hand, surging up and down, in what she thought must be the most embarrassing way possible. She wondered if Mike could see her pussy, peeping between her thighs, but decided he couldn't, thank goodness, even when her bottom squirmed like that.

But he had said all those things about how he would *inspect* her. The thought made her kick her feet, still bound together by the jeans he had stripped down all the way to her feet before he upended her over his knee. Kicking her feet did no good at all, of course, because Mike had her bottom exactly where he wanted it with his left hand on her back and his right leg firmly over both of hers. It did draw a rebuke from her daddy though. "You'll learn not to kick like that, sweetheart," Mike said in a grim voice, as if he really didn't want to have to punish Darla so severely but felt he had no choice. His hand came down hard, again and again.

"I'm sorry, daddy!" Darla wailed. "I'll obey you! Please! It hurts so much!"

"I'm glad to hear it," Mike said in the same grim tone, and kept spanking. "Maybe that will teach you the lesson you need. Little girls need to have stern lessons sometimes, if they want to grow up to be good citizens."

Darla's bottom burned like she had sat on a jellyfish, but her face seemed to burn even more at the idea that she had forfeited the right to be thought of as an adult. Mike's suggestion that she must go back to the beginning made her heart rebel again, and she kicked her feet defiantly, and tried in vain to twist her left arm around to grab some part of him.

"Hold. Still." Mike said, and delivered two hard spanks to the center of Darla's backside to accompany the words.

As if something inside her gave in at that point and yielded to his will for her to succumb to the notion of

herself as a naughty little girl under his care and guidance, Darla felt her body relax even as, under his firm, correcting hand, her poor bottom kept doing the uncontrollable squirmy dance that must show Mike his spanking had succeeded in giving her a lesson she would remember every time she had to put her panties on for the next day or so. She lay, sobbing, over her daddy's knee, as he finally stopped punishing her and began to rub her bottom gently.

"There," he said, with a note of satisfaction in his voice. "Are you going to try to be a good girl now?"

"Yes, daddy," Darla whimpered. Suddenly she found herself wondering in a very different way about what she had seen in the Selecta video. "Daddy?" she asked, as Mike held the roundness of her glowing bottom in his enormous hand.

"Yes, sweetheart?" He sounded a little distracted, for some reason.

"What's a special lesson?"

Mike cleared his throat. "You'll have to wait and see about that. It's a kind of big-girl training that gets you ready to have a mature relationship with a man who can guide you the way I do. You're definitely not getting one today, because you're not ready."

Darla felt her brow furrow at this unexpected answer. "I don't understand, daddy," she said. "What do you mean by a *mature relationship*?"

"I know you don't understand yet, sweetheart. Part of the DNLG program involves making sure that girls like you are ready to find a husband who will guide you with his firm hand in every way, as soon after you graduate from the program as possible."

Darla had no idea how to respond to this news, because so many conflicting emotions now roiled in what felt like her entire body—including, unfortunately, between her legs.

"Selecta doesn't play matchmaker, or anything like

that," Mike continued, "but it does form client relationships with men who qualify as disciplinarians, and it sends them listings of the girls who are about to come out of its correctional programs. Alright, sweetheart. Let's get you into your pretty blue pinafore."

He stood her up, carefully holding onto her as she almost fell when the blood rushed from her head. "Ow!" Darla exclaimed as her bottom jiggled. She tried to get a look at her rear end over her left shoulder, but failed. "Is it very red, daddy?" she asked, not knowing why the thought it might be seemed to make her feel strangely proud.

"Yes, sweetheart," Mike said. "Very red. You'll have to sit on a cushion to eat lunch and lie on your tummy to watch football this afternoon."

"Oh, do you watch football?" Darla said. She never did, herself, but she had always thought it would be nice to watch with a man who could explain it to her—like a daddy. She felt yet another blush creep across her face at that thought.

# CHAPTER FOUR

Darla did lie on her tummy, on the floor of Mike's living room, to watch the game. Whether because of the severity of the spanking he had given her or because she really had begun to see the wisdom of the program, she behaved herself very well, listening with adorable curiosity as Mike explained about the difference between lateral and forward passes.

At bedtime, she had her first inspection. After dinner Mike said, "Alright, Darla, go ahead into your room and get undressed. I'll be in to inspect you in a moment. Hang your pinafore up in your closet and put your underwear in the hamper. Then lay your nighty out on your bed and stand next to it, with your hands on your head. While you wait, go ahead and take a look in the mirror at your bottom, and think about why it's got some pretty bruises from your daddy's hand."

Darla, who was indeed sitting on a cushion on the high-backed wooden chair, widened her eyes. It seemed for a moment like she might protest, but she said, "Yes, daddy," instead, and got up to go to the little bedroom where she had unpacked after lunch.

Mike put the dishes in the dishwasher, and washed his

hands.

He found Darla looking behind herself in the mirror atop her dresser, shifting her cute little backside to try to get a good look. She had her hands, as specified, atop her head, and Mike felt a not unpleasant swelling of his cock at the pretty sight of his naked little girl.

"How are you feeling back there?" Mike asked as he entered.

Darla turned her eyes to him with a frightened look on her face, as if in fear that if she said her bottom had stopped hurting so much he might spank her again. "Okay, daddy?"

"Do you understand why I had to spank you?" Mike went to Darla's little bed with the pink comforter and sat next to the short white nightgown she had laid out there.

"Yes, daddy," she said softly, turning to face him. Her sweet pussy, covered sparsely with soft brown curls, presented itself to his view.

"I'm going to ask you some embarrassing questions, now, sweetheart," he said, "about your pussy."

"Oh, daddy!" Darla cried. "Why?"

"Two reasons. First, we need to know about your sexual experiences, to make sure we're adjusting the program for you in the right way. Second, you need to keep learning that you're not allowed to have secrets from your daddy. When you broke the law, you showed that you need a guardian who will inspect every part of you, even on the inside."

Darla's brow furrowed in consternation, but she gave a little nod.

"Have you had a man's cock inside you here?" Mike asked, reaching out with the upturned fingers of his right hand and very lightly pushing the middle two between Darla's trim thighs until he could feel the parting of her private lips, under the crisp brown hair.

She gave a soft little whimper, and nodded sharply. "Yes, daddy," she whispered.

"More than one, Darla?" With those two fingers, Mike began to rub very gently.

She shook her head. "No, daddy."

"Who was he?"

"He was my high school boyfriend. We... on my eighteenth birthday, we... did it. And a few times after that, before he left for the army."

"Did you love him?" Mike asked.

"I don't think I really did, even though I thought I did," Darla replied with a sigh, as Mike felt the wetness begin to come onto his fingertips. "He was nice, but, well, you know, almost too nice."

"I do know, sweetheart," Mike said. "That's why you're here with me. You need guidance, and you need it most of all where your little pussy is concerned. Did you come, with the cock inside?" He rubbed her a little harder, found her clit for the first time, and Darla gave a little moan as if at the extremity of the sensation.

She shook her head. "He tried to make me come with his hand and... you know... with his mouth..." Darla seemed to find this last part more embarrassing than anything else, as if her boyfriend hadn't taught her about how tasting a sweet eighteen-year-old pussy could represent a dominant form of enjoyment.

"But you only pretended to come?" Mike asked.

"Yes, daddy," she breathed. She had begun to move her hips in helpless, jerky little motions against Mike's fingers.

"But when you touch yourself, you come, don't you, sweetheart? I can tell."

"Yes, daddy." She gave a little giggle at that. The sound made Mike's heart feel light.

Mike pulled his fingers away. "Turn around," he said, "and touch your toes, with your feet spread just a little wider than your shoulders."

Darla made a frustrated little sound; Mike couldn't tell whether it was because he had stopped fondling her pussy

or because of the humiliation implied by the position he had commanded.

"Do I have to, daddy?" she asked, but it seemed like something new had entered the tone she used to respond to him in the negative—something Mike thought he might even call *playful*.

"Yes, you have to, sweetheart. Daddy needs to inspect you thoroughly. Hurry up and do as I say, or I might feel like I have to take your temperature the old-fashioned way, or even make sure things are working smoothly there, inside your bottom."

Looking up at her, he saw she knew exactly what he meant, and he guessed that she understood very well that both those things might well play a role in her life in the very near future. She closed her eyes for a moment, then turned around and bent at the waist, spreading her feet sluggishly at the same time. Her knees bent as her hands traveled down, so that her legs could stay more or less relaxed, though of course her bottom, with its lingering— if not very severe—bruises stretched out delightfully. Between her cheeks Darla showed him a wrinkly little hole, arousingly visible over her adorable fig of a pussy, where the pink inner lips now appeared very sweetly to her daddy's eyes.

Mike laid the tip of his index finger lightly on Darla's bottom-hole. She started, and began to straighten up, but he said, "Shh. Daddy will touch you here when he thinks it's necessary. Did your boyfriend ever put his cock in here, sweetheart?"

"No," Darla gasped.

"Did he ever ask to do it?"

"N-no… I mean, he n-never even… you know, I never… with my mouth, or anything."

Mike's cock had become very hard now, as he suppressed the urge to push his finger inside her cute bottom. Then he had to suppress the even greater urge to unbutton his jeans, pull them down, and slide into the

eighteen-year-old pussy that he could tell from the delicious aroma it was giving off would welcome him inside, before he told Darla that the time had come for her to begin her anal training, and he lubed her up for her first lesson.

But he said, "It's good to hear that, Darla. It sounds like he wasn't the right sort of man to take you in hand the way I'm going to teach you about. The right man will teach you to please him with your mouth and your little anus, but those are very special lessons that your daddy knows how to get you ready for."

Mike paused to gauge her reaction to this embarrassing news about what her time with him had in store for her most private places. Darla said nothing, but he could hear her breathing coming in aroused little pants. He smiled.

Removing his finger from her little rose, he cupped her pussy very lightly with his hand. Darla gave a little sighing moan half of pleasure and, he thought, half of frustration.

"Do you remember what I said about playing with yourself, Darla?"

"Yes, daddy," she said in a tiny sob.

"What did I say, sweetheart?"

"I'm not allowed to touch my pussy." Her voice sounded so adorably strained that Mike almost decided to make her come right then and there, bending over in front of him.

"Except?"

"Except when you give me permission, daddy."

"That's right. If you're a good girl for me tomorrow, I'll give you permission tomorrow night, and you can give this little pussy a nice big climax." He rubbed firmly, and Darla cried out. "Daddy will watch you do it, to make sure you're giving yourself as much pleasure as you can."

"Oh, no…" Darla moaned, though it wasn't really a protest as much as an expression of forlorn dismay. She had begun to see exactly what Mike wanted her to see—for the next six months, in his house, privacy was a thing

of the past for her.

He took his hand away reluctantly. "My fingers are very wet, Darla," he said softly.

"Sorry, daddy," she whispered.

"That's alright, sweetheart. When your daddy inspects you, it's natural to feel those big-girl feelings. It shows that you're starting to be ready for the right man to take you in hand and enjoy you, and make your little pussy feel good. And of course when daddy gives permission for you to play with yourself, it'll be even more natural to get wet down there, and to make the special noises girls make when their panties are down and they're learning about their bodies. But it's high time you learned that you and your daddy—and, when he comes along, the right man—must keep those feelings for the times you're allowed to feel big-girl pleasure. That's why I'll whip you with my belt if I catch you masturbating without permission. Do you understand?"

"Yes, daddy. I think so." She sounded hesitant, but that was only natural, Mike thought.

"Alright, sweetheart. You may go ahead and put on your nightgown. Then we'll go to the bathroom and you can pee for me."

Darla stood up, casting him a woeful look over her shoulder.

"None of that attitude, Darla," Mike said warningly. "You need to get used to this right now."

Just down the hall lay her bathroom.

"Hold your nighty up all the way, so daddy can see," he said as she sat on the toilet. He kept his eyes there between her legs, not needing to look up to know that Darla's face wore an expression of red-cheeked dismay. At last the golden stream rushed out with its soft *hiss* into the bowl's water. "There you go, good girl," Mike said approvingly. Now he did look into Darla's eyes, and found a proud little expression there despite the blush that suffused her face.

He watched her wipe, wash her hands, and brush her

teeth. Then he said, "Time for a bedtime story?"

Darla's brow furrowed, perhaps as much at the questioning tone as at what Mike knew must be the surprising news that her daddy intended to engage in this sort of daddy behavior, too.

"Okay, daddy," she said a little uncertainly. "What kind of story?"

"You tell me," Mike said with a smile, "and I'll make it up."

Darla's eyes lit up at that. "Really? I always wanted a daddy who could make up stories that way!" Just as suddenly as her fleeting joy had come, though, it seemed to disappear. Her face now seemed to say, with its puzzled expression, that perhaps she hadn't even known until that moment that she had wanted that kind of daddy, or any daddy.

"Don't worry, sweetheart," Mike said. "You're going to feel a lot of unexpected things over the next few days and weeks." She had turned her eyes to the floor, but now she raised them again to Mike's face. She ventured a smile, and Mike smiled back. He put his arms around her and gave her a quick hug, tickled her ribs to make her giggle. She did giggle, and let herself be led back to her room and tucked into her bed.

"Once upon a time," Mike said softly, "there was a…"

Darla yawned hugely, clearly realizing how very tired she was in the space of a millisecond. "Sorry, daddy. A princess?"

"A princess," Mike said.

"Who was naughty," Darla said firmly, if very softly, and then yawned again. "And got… spanked."

Mike grinned. "Once upon a time," he began again, slowly and quietly, "there was a princess who was naughty and got…"

But Darla had already closed her eyes.

# CHAPTER FIVE

Darla woke the next morning to find Mike rubbing her shoulder gently. "Mmm," she said. "What time?"

"Time to get up for work," he said in a patient voice that reassured her that thanks to him she hadn't overslept the way she usually did.

*Not a dream, then?* Not the strangest dream ever, that she wore a blue little-girl dress with a pinafore after her spanking to come to her new daddy's house? That she watched football lying on her tummy because her bottom hurt so much, because her daddy had punished her?

That her daddy had inspected her at bedtime, and made her feel so funny, and watched her pee, and told her a story—or started to, because Darla realized with a little blush, looking up into Mike's eyes, that she had fallen instantly into a dreamless refreshing sleep.

"Can we finish the story tonight, daddy?" she asked shyly.

"Sure, sweetheart," Mike said. "Now get going. I don't like to hurry at all. We've got plenty of time to get you to work, but only if you get yourself into gear the way you're going to learn to here in my house."

So Darla did. She was used to moving quickly in the

morning, but that was because she always overslept. It felt weird to move quickly because her daddy didn't want to feel rushed. It almost seemed like a completely new way to think about what morning was, to be able to sit and have an English muffin with peanut butter at the table while her daddy drank coffee and read the paper on his tablet.

Before they got up to go to the car, Mike said, "Now, Darla, do you remember about using the bathroom at work?"

She felt her face get hot. "Yes, daddy."

"Tell me." Mike's patient voice held a bit of sternness, as if he had heard in her tone Darla's reluctance to remember this part.

"I have to text you when I want to go to the bathroom."

"And then?"

Darla felt her brow furrow. "I don't really have to, do I? Please, daddy?"

"You really have to, Darla. You're headed for a spanking before work, this way. Tell me."

Her voice came out in a little squeak. "I have to make a video of myself, and send it to you."

"That's right, sweetheart. You'll get used to it."

But Darla couldn't see how she could ever get used to it, and she resolved that moment to pretend that she didn't have to go to the bathroom all day.

At least it felt good to be wearing her regular work clothes, a black skirt and a pink top, with black tights over her regular beige panties. Darla had never thought she'd be grateful to be allowed to wear adult underwear. The white cotton little-girl panties with the pink frills around the waist and legs weren't terrible, she supposed—especially since they were hidden under the pinafore—but putting them on and taking them off had made her blush terribly.

Then again, so little seemed *not* to make her blush about this new life that had already started to seem a great deal more normal than she had imagined it ever could.

When Mike, dropping her off at the car dealership where Darla served as a cashier, patted her on the shoulder and said, "Be a good girl for me today," she blushed.

How could she not, since she knew what would happen that night if Mike decided she *had* been a good girl? The image of herself in bed, with her daddy watching… it sent an awful shiver down her spine that Darla found even worse because something in that shiver *didn't* feel as awful as she thought it should.

For the first hour of work, sitting next to her fellow cashier, Joanne and doing all the normal things— announcing to the car owners in the lobby that their oil changes were done, telling them to wave their phones at the pay-point, saying "Thanks so much, Mr. So-and-so. You have a great day now!"—Darla fought the strangest urge to tell Joanne that she had a daddy now. She had no idea why she would want to tell her coworker, who wasn't even really a friend, and didn't even know about Darla's little run-ins with the law. But sitting there in grownup clothes, doing grownup things, made Darla feel like she had a secret, and she'd never been very good with secrets. Plus, something about knowing Mike was somewhere waiting for her to text about the bathroom made her feel special, just as much as it made her blush.

For the second hour of work, she waged a mental battle against her bladder. Despite having resolved that she would lie to Mike about the bathroom, part of her knew that the idea was foolish, and made her simply not want to go to the bathroom instead, as if she could prove to him that she really could go a full day without peeing, so he could just forget about the texting and the humiliating video.

So by 10:30, Darla had begun to shift so uncomfortably in her chair as her bladder commanded her attention that she felt sure Joanne would notice. At least, she thought wildly, it was happening this early in the day. If it had happened at the end of the day she could imagine trying to

hold it, and then peeing in her panties in Mike's car. What would Mike do?

*He'd spank me, wouldn't he? Of course my daddy would spank me, if my pee came out all over the car seat.* Darla couldn't believe she had imagined it, and she couldn't stop imagining it, as she tried to hold a single agonizing Kegel, knowing she could never last another minute, let alone another six hours.

"Darla?" Joanne asked, looking at her from the chair next to hers. "What's wrong? You're bright red. Are you feeling alright?"

Darla bit down on the inside of her cheek until she tasted blood, and she knew her face looked like a mask of pain. "I'm okay," she squeaked. "I just need the bathroom."

Joanne's face took on a bemused look, as if incredulous that Darla would have waited until, like a bashful little girl, she reached the highly embarrassing state in which she now found herself. "Go ahead," she said. "I'll hold down the fort."

Just as Darla was getting up, the text came in from Mike.

*How are you doing, sweetheart? Do you need to pee?*

On the toilet, literally groaning with relief as her pee gushed out and terribly grateful that the bathroom was a small one, for a single person, Darla wrote back with trembling thumbs.

*Just fine, daddy. No, I don't usually need to go to the bathroom at work.*

Lying would make it worse. Of course it would make it worse. But… what else could Darla do?

When she returned to the cashier's desk, it seemed like the little incident before Darla had gotten up had put

Joanne in mind of exactly the sort of thing Darla would much rather her coworker didn't talk about.

"Have you heard about the new correctional programs?" she asked.

"No," Darla lied, trying to keep her response short and entirely uninterested.

"It's just that I saw this thing in my newsfeed last week, and you made me think of it just now," Joanne continued breezily. She clearly had no idea how close to home she had hit. "These new nonviolent offender programs are allowed to do *crazy* stuff. Like not let you go to the bathroom, or make you go in your clothes, or make you call your parole officer or whatever to get permission."

Darla had never been so grateful to have a mechanic come in and tell her some guy's car was ready.

After she'd taken care of the customer, though, Joanne, clearly fascinated by the topic, picked right up where she'd left off. "They can punish you any way they *want*," she intoned in a lower, more confidential voice. "Like, spanking and paddling and things. Enemas, even." Joanne giggled nervously.

"*Enemas*?" Darla couldn't help responding. Mike wouldn't, would he? *Of course he would*, her mind answered back.

"This one girl? They said she had to take off her clothes every night so that this guy could *inspect* her."

Darla didn't think her face had ever felt hotter. To her own astonishment, she said, "But… I mean, wouldn't that teach her… I don't know, to feel ashamed of herself, or… something?"

"I guess," Joanne said a little doubtfully. "But I'd rather go to jail, wouldn't you?"

"Mmm," Darla said noncommittally.

"Well, the girl in the story I saw agreed with you, I guess. I'll give you that. She said that she learned her lesson, or something. She said that she hadn't ever realized that she needed someone to take care of her, and to tell

her how to behave. The company probably planted the story." Joanne busied herself with some paperwork.

Part of Darla wanted to end the conversation, gratefully, there. But, as if it might make up for lying to her daddy, she found herself saying, "What? Like a boyfriend who… you know…" She groped for a phrase, and found that the one Mike had used the day before fit better than anything else she could have picked. "…takes you in hand?"

Joanne shot her a funny look, as if Darla's words had touched a chord in her that had motivated her to talk about the correctional stuff in the first place and had now risen higher in her mind—as if Darla had named a desire that Joanne too possessed. "I guess," was all she said, her own cheeks becoming rather pink.

∙ ∙ ∙ ∙ ∙ ∙ ∙

Mike didn't text again all day, and Darla went out to the curb when she saw him pull up, thinking with relief that she must have gotten away with her lie. But as soon as she got into the car, she could tell that she had landed into a heap of trouble with her daddy. She looked at his chiseled jaw, set forward with precision, and realized that he had turned the car off and had made no move to start it again, and she felt her stomach seem to sink down lower than the car seat.

"Darla," Mike said softly but with so much authority that it made her shudder, "you can make the lesson I have to teach you this evening a little less severe if you confess right now."

"Daddy…" Darla started, her hands quaking with fear in her lap. She wanted to confess. She didn't want any lesson at all, let alone a severe one, but she couldn't bear to say that she had lied, because that would mean that she would definitely get punished. Tears leaked from her eyes. Maybe she could convince him she hadn't lied?

But now he turned to her with an angry and disappointed look in his eye.

"Daddy, wh-what are you going to do?"

"That depends on whether you confess, sweetheart," he said levelly. "How many times did you go to the bathroom today?"

"Twice," Darla whispered.

"Did you do as I'd told you to do?"

"No, daddy."

Mike nodded once, sharply. "I didn't come to your workplace to make a scene and embarrass you despite knowing that you lied to me. I want you to understand, though, that the next time you disobey me, or disrespect the rules I've made, I will do that, and I will make you change into your little-girl clothes right there at work."

"No! Please, daddy!"

"Yes, sweetheart. Today, because you confessed, I'm only going to take away the hair between your legs and put you in a diaper."

"What?!" *Oh, no. Please, no.* "Please, daddy. I'll be good. I promise."

"You'll wear a diaper to work tomorrow, under your dress, and you will pee in it. I will come get you at your lunch hour and change you here in the car. Then, if you're a good girl and pee in your diaper in the afternoon, too, you will be allowed to change into big-girl panties when you get home tomorrow evening."

# CHAPTER SIX

Darla cried all the way home, pleading with him not to put her in diapers, but Mike could tell from her tears that the punishment would be very effective indeed. He had felt some skepticism when he read the part in the Selecta training manual about diaper discipline, but he could already see that it would work for his little girl. Mike didn't like making her cry, of course, but judging from her reaction the day before about him watching her pee, and now at the thought of having her pussy bared and then covered up in a diaper instead of panties, he could tell that the training manual had it right.

*Giving up control of her toileting is an essential part of any offender's naughty-girl program. The correctional officer must be decisive and strict. Begin by telling your naughty girl that she must request permission to go to the bathroom, and find a way to verify that she has not gone there without permission. At home, watch her urinate, and make it clear that you have the right to see that she takes good care of her diaper area, wiping her there yourself if you think it appropriate. Be prepared to mete out diaper discipline if she violates any of your rules in this regard: shave her pubic hair to make her feel more keenly that you have withdrawn her adult privileges,*

*and put her in diapers for at least a night and most of a day, requiring her to wet her diaper and be changed by you at least twice. You'll find that your diaper girl learns very quickly to pay closer attention to your instructions. If you're satisfied with her conduct at that point, don't hesitate to reward her sexually: diaper girls often need to understand just how strongly their erotic feelings are tied to the right man's control of their most basic bodily functions.*

When they reached Mike's house, only a five-minute drive from Darla's car dealership, she turned to him one last time. "Please, daddy," she said, her eyes bright with tears. "Please, no diapers. Please, just… just take away… you know, my hair down there? I promise I'll text and make the videos tomorrow."

"Darla, sweetheart," he replied slowly and steadily. "I have to make it clear to you just how serious a matter this is. I need to treat you like a little girl until I see that you can behave with obedience and respect the way a law-abiding grownup woman does. Don't make me spank you, too, for trying to get out of your discipline. Get into the house and go to your room. Take off all your clothes and wait for me to call you to come to the bathroom for your bath."

She made an adorable, heart-rending boo-boo face, and then turned away, unbuckled her seatbelt, and began to climb out of the car.

· · · · · · ·

Ten minutes later, Mike knocked on her door, and opened it to find her naked, her hands clasped in front of her pussy, her delightful little nipples standing up on the tiny, pert handfuls of her breasts. He had to concentrate hard on the matter at hand to resist taking the little peaches into his own hands. The urge to give Darla a sexual reward just for stripping naked as instructed rose a little higher and, yes, harder than he had anticipated.

But instead he said gruffly, "We'll start by clipping your hair down there with scissors. Then we'll put you in a warm bath to make your pussy easier to shave. You'll lie on a towel while I get you nice and smooth."

"And then?" Darla asked, her voice a little hopeful.

"Then the diaper, sweetheart."

The boo-boo face returned, and a tear trickled down her cheek, but the threat of a spanking seemed to have ensured a little obedience. She preceded him down the hall to the bathroom, where he had laid out two thicknesses of fluffy white towels, as well as bringing a low stool for himself. Steam from the bath rose into the air and fogged the mirror in the white-and-green tiled room.

"Lie down and spread your knees nice and wide, sweetheart," Mike said. He picked up the scissors from the vanity counter.

"Like this, daddy?" Darla asked meekly, lying down and separating her feet.

"Nope. Lift your knees up and take them in your hands. Show me everything." In Darla's face, Mike saw the extremity of the embarrassment she felt at assuming the humiliatingly exposed position, in which Mike had his best view yet of her pussy's sweet pink secrets and the little rose of her anus, still lightly covered by her brown grownup curls.

*Not for long.*

"Can this be my inspection for tonight, too, daddy?" Darla asked in a sweeter tone than she had yet used that evening. This form of discipline really did seem to have a very salutary effect on her, Mike reflected.

"You're forgetting that I'm going to change your diaper later, sweetheart. That'll be your inspection." Mike didn't think she'd actually forgotten, on reflection: she seemed still to be hoping that if she were extra-obedient for the baring, maybe he would relent about the diaper. If so, she had another think coming, because Mike's hard cock had long since decided that putting Darla in a diaper needed to

happen tonight, and the reward tomorrow.

He sat on the low stool, bent down to take the first tuft of her pubic hair in the fingers of his left hand, then carefully cut it off low down, near her skin. Darla gave a little whimper at the feeling.

"Have you ever thought about shaving yourself down here, sweetheart?" Mike asked as he continued to another tuft.

"Y-yes?" Darla confessed. "I mean, doesn't everyone think about that?"

"I'm not sure," Mike said. "I guess a lot of girls do, anyway. The right man for you might well have you shave or wax regularly for him." Darla didn't really have a great deal of hair on her pussy, so the job was going very quickly; Mike started to trim the few hairs around her anus now. Darla made a startled, embarrassed kind of noise that made Mike's cock even stiffer. He couldn't be sure, but he thought that he had begun to smell a musky scent alongside the soapy smells from the tub.

"Waxing!" Darla said, with a shiver, as if trying to cover her reaction to Mike's touch around her rosy little bottom-hole. "Why, daddy?"

"Why waxing?"

"Why does the right man want me not to have any hair there?"

"Go ahead and get into the tub, now, sweetheart," Mike said.

"Okay, daddy," Darla replied, beginning to get up from the floor.

As she stepped into the tub, her pussy already looking deliciously bare and innocent, Mike reflected, "Because the kind of man who can take you in hand likes to know that he gets to say whether you can cover your pussy. When he takes your panties down to have big-girl time with you in your bed, he likes to see that you look the way he decided you should, in the place where he puts his cock to enjoy himself."

A shiver seemed to go through Darla at that, despite the warmth of the tub. Mike noticed that her hand seemed to have drifted down between her legs. He decided to pretend she wasn't contemplating mischief, though he felt quite sure his little description of the way the right man would fuck her had stirred some rather intense sensations down there.

"Isn't that…" Darla swallowed hard. Mike watched her try to figure out what to say next, as if at a loss at how she could protest against the arousal she clearly felt when he talked about her submissive sexual future. He took a washcloth, then, and without any preliminaries to the peremptory act, he tugged her naughty hand out of the way and began to soap his little girl between her legs.

"Oh, daddy, please," she sighed, blushing. When Mike said nothing, she whispered, "What are you doing, daddy?"

"I'm getting you ready for the razor," he said gently. "We're going to get the hair nice and soft, and then I'll be able to get you nice and smooth in your diaper area."

"Mmm…" was all Darla could manage then, because Mike had started to use his middle finger, through the washcloth, to emphasize the overarching lesson that daddies get to say about when little girls' pussies feel nice.

"Are you going to be a good girl for me tonight, after I bare your cute little pussy?" he asked softly. "Are you going to pee in your diaper like a good girl?"

"Oh, God…" Darla murmured. "Oh, God, daddy, I'm… I'm going…"

Mike looked into her face, which had gone very red. She had shut her eyes tightly. Her hands clenched and unclenched, and every muscle in her adorable naked body seemed to tense. Mike almost decided to give her this climax, just because she seemed to be learning to behave herself so well.

He knew, though, that it would be counterproductive in the end. Much better to teach her that orgasms were for girls who really demonstrated they had learned their

lessons. He took the washcloth away and started to soap her tummy instead.

"Daddy!" Darla wailed. "Please?"

"Not now, sweetheart," Mike said. "Remember that you would have been allowed to play with yourself tonight if you hadn't been naughty today. If you're a good little diaper girl tonight and tomorrow, you'll masturbate for me tomorrow night after inspection."

She made her boo-boo face, but she nodded, too. Then, after a pause in which the only sounds were the splashes of the washcloth and Darla's still-labored breathing, "Daddy?"

"Yes, sweetheart?"

"Does your cock get hard when you touch me? Between my legs, I mean?"

The question sounded so very innocent that Mike didn't know how to respond. If Darla had asked it in a wicked way, he thought he would have spanked her— maybe even hauled her out of the bath and spanked her that instant. But she seemed really to want to know, as if she had regressed in her thoughts and feelings to a point where her emotions all looked different to her, and she wanted to try to put them together anew.

"Yes, sweetheart, it does," Mike finally said, looking into her sweet brown eyes.

"Do you want to put it inside me, when it gets hard?" She gave a tiny smile at that, as if she wanted him to know that if he thought it was a good idea to fuck her, she would try to be a good little girl, and let him enjoy her young body however he liked.

"Sweetheart, we just met yesterday," Mike protested, his cock truly so hard that he had to shift on the stool.

"I know, daddy," Darla said, sounding a little abashed. "I'm sorry. I just… well, I feel like I'm starting to understand what it means to be a good girl, and you keep telling me about what the right man will do with my body—you know, in my mouth and my bottom and my

pussy, when he comes to my bed and pulls my panties down. I kind of want to feel what it will feel like. Are you allowed to do that?"

Mike realized that his own breathing had become a little harsher.

"I'm going to tell you the truth, Darla, and then we're not going to go any further with this talk tonight. We're going to get your pussy bare, we're going to put you in your diaper, and you're going to show me you can be my diaper girl. We're not going to talk about having sex."

"Okay, daddy," she replied meekly. "What's the truth?"

Mike took a deep breath as he decided he mustn't beat around the bush, but should use the grownup terms, to emphasize the gravity of the matter to Darla. "The truth is that I'm allowed to fuck you, if you consent."

"But…"

Mike knew Darla was about to say that she consented—was probably about to beg him to fuck her. God, how he wanted to do that right now: to get in the tub himself, turn her over, and ride her like a cute little pony, holding her hips firmly until he shot his seed deep into her sweet pussy.

Instead, he did what he knew he had to do. "Not another word, Darla, or you'll have a spanking before I put the diaper on."

# CHAPTER SEVEN

So he *could* fuck her, if he wanted to. But he didn't want to.

Or... Darla thought about what he had said, about how they weren't going to talk about it anymore.

Maybe her daddy did want to fuck her, but just as he had stopped playing with her pussy through the washcloth, her daddy wanted her to understand that if he fucked her, it would be because *he* wanted to and not because *she* did. What was wrong with her, that made that submissive thought send a quiver of arousal shooting out from her pussy and seem to fill her midsection with fiery light?

"Okay, sweetheart," he said, taking a fluffy towel from the bar next to the tub. "Time to get out of the tub." He handed her the towel. "Once you're dry, go ahead and lie on your back on the towel on the floor, with your legs spread just like before."

She snuggled into the towel, which smelled fresh and felt warm. The scent of the detergent was different from the one she was used to, and that seemed to Darla to emphasize in some obscure, but somehow also very nice, way that her daddy had begun to take her in hand. The shivery feeling she had gotten the very first time she heard

that phrase, the one she had tried so hard to pretend she didn't feel, only seemed to grow, now that Darla knew what taking in hand meant: washcloths between your legs, a shaved pussy, and a promise that if you were good you'd be allowed to play with yourself while your daddy watched to make sure you were doing it right.

Thinking about all that, and feeling how the shivery feeling had seemed to move rather boldly into the inexperienced pussy that her daddy would now shave, she had fallen still, but Mike said, "No dawdling, Darla. Do as I've said. It's time to bare your little pussy, so lie down and open yourself up."

*Open yourself up*. Darla obeyed, putting the fluffy towel, now a little damp, back on the bar from which Mike had taken it and feeling despite the warmth of the bathroom a tremble go through her body to be naked once again in front of her daddy. That never seemed to go away—the feeling that something about being daddy's good girl involved having to be his naughty little girl, too, only with her naughtiness under daddy's control.

Blushing, she raised her knees and took them into her hands again, opening herself for her daddy's eyes, and the shaving lotion he began to rub into her pussy so delicately that it was even worse than when he had soaped her with the washcloth and made her think about whether he might be getting hard, and whether he might like to put that hardness inside his good little girl's pussy, once he had bared it. She tried to look at the white ceiling with the recessed light, but she couldn't help herself: she looked down her body to see Mike's handsome face as, intent on his task, he began carefully to use the pink plastic razor on her most private places.

Nor could Darla help following his gaze and catching sight of her own pussy, as she had never seen it, for she had always found it terribly shameful to look at herself even on those rare occasions when her posture might permit it. But her daddy's commands had put her in a

position now where Darla, her knees held firmly back in her own hands, could see the forbidden places, and see how Mike had lathered them for their final baring.

Each stroke of the razor took some of the lotion away and left a smooth strip behind, and every time Darla couldn't suppress a little whimper at the sensation and then the sight of herself, being prepared to wear a diaper, to be her daddy's diaper girl tonight and tomorrow. She had no idea why the thought of peeing in a diaper could both make her face go hot with shame and raise in her some of the filthiest thoughts she could ever remember having.

She found, as Mike continued the shaving ritual calmly, relentlessly, and without speaking, that she couldn't get rid of one terrible mental picture above all.

In her mind's eye, her daddy decided to teach his diaper girl the sternest possible lesson. He decided to take her bottom's virginity with his hard cock. Under him the diaper girl cried out that even though it hurt she would learn to be his good girl. He said, as he rode the little bottom, that her submission pleased him, and she must have him there in her bottom every night from now on, after her bedtime story, to help her fall asleep.

She looked at his face again, and saw on it a concern to make sure he wielded the razor with precision. The care he took with every detail of her training suddenly seemed to Darla to deserve no description better than it deserved the word *noble*. As soon as she had thought it, that her daddy had a nobility about him despite the many roughhewn parts of his personality, his chiseled chin and his strong cheekbones sent a tremor of desire through her that she had never felt for any man before.

"Alright, sweetheart," Mike said, wiping the last of the lotion onto a washcloth. "I'm going to give you a washcloth and have you rinse your pussy, now. Be careful, though. No funny business. Daddy will be watching, and he'll put you over this stool and paddle you with the bath

brush if you get naughty."

"Okay, daddy," Darla said in a quivery voice. "I'll be good." Her hand trembled as she reached it between her legs to take the washcloth, soaked in warm water, that her daddy brought her.

"Rinse that pussy well, Darla," Mike said. "I don't want any complaints that you're itchy in your diaper because you left some stubble there."

Darla tried hard not to whimper as she ran the washcloth, which felt shamefully lovely, back and forth.

"Yes, daddy," she said.

"It's just about the cutest little pussy I ever saw," her daddy said. "Sometime soon I think I'll have a little taste of it, to see if it tastes as sweet as it looks."

"Oh, daddy," Darla said, as of course the pussy her daddy referred to fluttered at his words. He must be playing, now, right? "Wouldn't you like to do that right now?"

"No, sweetheart," Mike said sadly, turning his attention from her task with the washcloth between her legs to her face for a moment. "Daddy has to punish his little diaper girl tonight. Maybe I'll taste you tomorrow, after you show me how you play with yourself."

"If I'm a good girl tomorrow," Darla whispered.

Mike nodded. "That's right, sweetheart."

Oh, how she wanted to ask what she might have to do, to have him teach her a lesson with his cock. But he said, "Alright, that's enough. Your diaper is laid out on your bed. Go lie on top of it. I'll come in in a minute to put the baby powder on and do the diaper up."

In a kind of daze of erotic feeling, all her thoughts seeming to whirl inside her head around the pivot of somehow finding a way to get her daddy to show her his cock, Darla let Mike help her up from the floor. He gave her a pat on her bottom to let her know she must get going, and she obediently padded out of the bathroom and down the little hall to her room.

The feeling of bareness between her legs as she walked took a great deal of getting used to. Not only did the sensation seem greater in her pussy even as the air touched places it hadn't touched so directly before, but the idea that her daddy had brought that sensation about by taking control of his little girl's pussy, baring it to show her that her most private places would look the way he wanted them to look, would not go away.

In her room she found that her little bed had on it a big square of thick white fabric that bore along one edge the word *SELECTA*. Of course the correctional company would make diapers for the program, wouldn't they? Darla wondered with a blush how many naughty little girls were wearing diapers tonight because their correctional officers had decided they needed to learn a lesson in acting their age.

For a moment Darla just stood and looked at the diaper, trying to figure out how her face could be blazing like the sun and her pussy shamefully warm and wet at the same time. The fear that Mike would see that arousal seemed to make it even worse. What was wrong with her?

Suddenly she had an idea that seemed so naughty and wicked it sent her scurrying onto the bed, on her back just as Mike had told her, hoping to get the terrible moment over with so that she could be sure she wouldn't do thing she had just imagined. But the diaper itself, with its innocent white softness, seemed only to make the wickedness in her bottom and her pussy grow.

Mike stood in the doorway, holding a pink and white container of baby powder and a glass of water. "Get your knees up, sweetheart," he said. "Show me where your diaper goes."

Darla obeyed, looking at her handsome daddy between her thighs as he approached, willing him to do up the Velcro fastenings on the diaper quickly so that she wouldn't say what she felt herself in such danger of saying.

Mike shook powder between her legs, to keep her bare

pussy nice and dry. It felt ticklish, and Darla gave a nervous giggle. "You're doing very well, sweetheart," he said encouragingly, as he put the powder down and pulled the diaper up and over her front. "Such a shame to cover up this sweet pussy, but someone has to get this diaper wet for me."

Then Darla blurted it out—the terrible thing. She couldn't help it. As she lowered her legs so that her calves and feet dangled over the edge of the bed, she whispered, "Daddy, if I suck your cock, it wouldn't be a reward, would it? Can I suck your cock while I go pee in my diaper?"

Well she certainly had managed to take her daddy aback for the first time. Mike straightened, took a step back. Darla wondered if there was a section in the manual called *When your naughty little girl asks to suck your cock.*

"That…" Mike said. Darla could see him trying to process his arousal with his care for her and the need to take her in hand. But she couldn't see how it might be wrong, to learn her diaper girl lesson with her daddy's penis in her mouth, struggling to please him, trying to make him come and put his special daddy stuff in her belly.

"Please, daddy? Maybe I could just see it, and touch it, to help me learn my lesson? Then if you want to make me suck it, you can do that because you get to say. See? I think I understand. I know it's kind of a treat to be allowed to see your cock, but isn't it also kind of a punishment to have to suck it and make you feel good? Shouldn't a firm daddy like you tell your little girl to take his cock in a place where it doesn't make her feel good whenever it gets hard? And…" She had started, and now it seemed she couldn't stop. "And maybe you should put it in my bottom, too, because that's even more like a punishment, isn't it?"

Mike started to shake his head, but not in the sort of severe negation a daddy might use to forbid something—rather in disbelief, it seemed to Darla, at what his little girl

had said. Desperate to have her way, desperate to see her daddy's penis, marveling that something could feel so wrong and so right at the same time, she compressed her lips into a tight line and felt her forehead crease.

At last Mike said, the decision and firmness coming back into his voice, "Not in your bottom tonight, sweetheart. But, yes, you'll suck my cock while you wet your diaper. Sit up and drink your water, now, and then daddy will take out his penis for you to make him feel good with your little mouth. Daddy will fuck your bottom another time."

# CHAPTER EIGHT

He picked up the glass of water from Darla's bureau and held it out to her as his diaper girl, her cute little grownup breasts contrasting so thrillingly with the white flannel that covered her around her hips and between her legs, sat up to take it. She looked at him very shyly now, as if not sure whether she really meant it about sucking his cock. Well, she had gone beyond the point of no return, hadn't she, now? She would have to do as she had said, and learn a very complicated lesson about her daddy's right to do whatever he wanted with his naughty little girl's body.

"I'm going to go sit in my den," Mike said. "When you're ready to suck my cock, you may come and join me there, sweetheart."

He sat in his easy chair and read a car magazine on his tablet, trying to concentrate on the latest models of the classic Ford pickup truck. After a hundred years of making them look more futuristic, the corporation, which Mike noticed with a smile was now part of the same conglomerate as Selecta, had returned to a style that resembled the original F-150 more closely than anything in more than a century had.

Mike usually salivated over any automotive development that brought out his nostalgia, but tonight he couldn't concentrate on either the pictures or the text, and he sat looking at the same page for two or three minutes.

"Daddy?" came the little voice from the doorway. "May I come in?"

Mike turned to see Darla standing there, shifting from foot to foot a little. Had she waited until she really had to go? *Good girl. Such a good girl.*

"Yes, sweetheart," Mike answered. "Come and kneel in front of daddy. He has something big and hard that you need to learn to please."

At his words Darla drew a gasping little breath, and Mike wondered if he had just sent some sort of tremor going between her thighs. She stepped quickly over to the chair, into the pool of light from the lamp on the table next to Mike's leather-covered easy chair. She knelt on the thick shag carpet, looking up at Mike with the boo-boo face.

That face drove him almost crazy with arousal knowing what would happen now, what he would put in her mouth and between those pouting lips. He stood up, beginning to unbuckle his belt and watching Darla's eyes widen as if in confusion as to what he would do with the belt once he had it unfastened.

"Have you ever seen a man's penis close up before, Darla? It sounds like that old boyfriend of yours didn't have you take a good look at his."

Darla shook her head, her brown ponytail swishing across her bare shoulders. Mike pulled down his jeans and his briefs and let them drop, as his hard cock sprang free, pointing straight at the face of his naughty little girl. She gave another tiny gasp and drew back a bit.

"Don't be frightened, sweetheart," Mike said. "I'll be as gentle with you as I can be, because you've decided to behave yourself." He sat back down. "Now, are you ready to wet your diaper?"

The boo-boo face returned. "I don't know, daddy. I think so?" Her eyes turned downward from Mike's face to his erection. "It's very big, daddy," she said. "Do I have to suck it?"

Mike felt a little smile play across his lips. "Who was it who asked to suck her daddy's penis, sweetheart?"

"Me," Darla whispered. She looked up at Mike with a furrowed brow, just a little glance, and then back down at his naked lap.

"You got your daddy very hard thinking about his little girl learning to be a good cocksucker, and now I guess I have to teach you that good girls don't tease their daddies that way. Get going, sweetheart. Suck the penis, and wet your diaper like a good girl."

Darla took a deep breath. Her eyes darted up to Mike's one final time, as if she needed to see resolution on his face—the confirmation that he would punish her now if she didn't please him so very shamefully with her mouth. Mike gave her a little nod, and a stern look: *Yes, you will have a spanking if you don't take daddy's hard cock in your little mouth this instant.*

She looked back down, bit her lip, finally opened her mouth a little, then more as she looked at the cock rising before her, as if realizing that she would have to hold her mouth very wide to do this naughty thing. Mike could hardly believe how much he now craved having that little face all the way down his cock, with Darla's nose buried in his wiry brown pubic hair, shamefully taking her daddy's balls deep because that was the way her daddy liked it.

Darla hesitated, still looking down anxiously at the cock, her mouth wide open. Mike couldn't resist: he put out both his hands, lifting them from the leather arms of the easy chair and reaching them toward Darla's head. Gently he gathered her ponytail in his right hand as with his left he encircled the back of her neck.

A little whimpering sound came from Darla, but she showed no sign of trying to pull away. Mike exerted a very

gentle pressure downward, toward his hard penis, and Darla didn't resist; her mouth engulfed him, and Mike couldn't suppress a little grunt at the extremity of the pleasure his cock found there as he sheathed himself halfway inside the pretty pink lips. Still being as gentle as he knew how, he began to move her head up and down, loving not just the velvety feeling around his manhood, but—almost as much—the sight of his good little girl doing her naughty duty.

Suddenly Darla's face turned bright red as her daddy fucked it, and Mike heard a little hissing sound from down below. He smiled. "There you go, sweetheart. See? Tomorrow when you wet your diaper at work, you can go to the bathroom and think about sucking daddy's cock, and that will help you go."

That thought, together with the sight of Darla's downcast eyes as she wet her diaper and the wonderful soft sensations only a girl's mouth can provide, made Mike push down a little, so that his cockhead went even deeper as her lips slid deliciously down the shaft. Darla made a little gagging sound, but Mike had to teach her, didn't he? He kept his naughty little girl's face down with his hands and said, "Daddy's going to come in your mouth, now, sweetheart. Get ready."

He held Darla's head still and used the give in the seat of his easy chair to pump his hips—once, twice, and then as Darla gave a startled sound his seed spurted, and he made her swallow it all, as his hips spasmed and the incredible pleasure of face-fucking a diaper girl ripped through him.

Still keeping her mouth full of cock with his right hand on her ponytail, Mike stroked her cheek with the knuckles of his left hand. "You asked to suck daddy's cock, didn't you? That's what you get, isn't it, sweetheart? When you suck daddy's cock, daddy gets to say."

He lifted her head, and she looked up at him, her eyes watering and her boo-boo face on. "Yes, daddy," she said,

bending down to give his cock a final little kiss. "Did it feel good?"

"It felt very good, sweetheart. You'll be daddy's little cocksucker from now on."

The pout turned into a mischievous little smile in an instant. "So I don't have to wear my diaper tomorrow?"

Mike frowned. "What makes you think that, Darla?"

Her brow furrowed. "I thought… Well, I kind of thought… that if…" Her voice trailed off, as she obviously could read the expression on her daddy's face.

"Darla, listen to me carefully."

"Yes, daddy." She had started to tremble a little.

"The next time you try to get out of a punishment by making daddy feel good, you're going to wind up lying over your bed with daddy's belt coming down on your bare backside to show you what a foolish thing that is to do. You'll make me feel good when I decide it's appropriate, from now on—now that you've consented to having my cock inside your young body, Selecta corporate policy says that I may exercise my sexual rights as I please. But I will also continue to be strict with you, so that you can graduate from the program and go on to find the right man to take you in hand permanently. You'll wear your diaper tonight, and you'll wear your diaper tomorrow. If you want your reward tomorrow night, you'd better not try to get out of it again. Now get going into your bedroom and get a fresh diaper out of your top drawer for me. Then lie on your bed. I'll come and change you in a moment."

He found her lying penitently as he had specified, clutching the diaper to her chest. "Daddy?" she said softly, as he leaned over her diaper area and began to unfasten the Velcro. "Will you fuck me tonight?"

"No, sweetheart," he said gently, looking into her eyes. "You're still being punished."

"But you want to fuck me, daddy?"

Mike felt his heart give a little leap. "Yes, Darla," he said. "Daddy wants very much to fuck his naughty little

girl."

"I'm sorry I was naughty," she said. "I understand about the diapers, I really do."

Mike had her wet one off, now, and he put it in the little pail he'd brought. He looked down at her adorable pussy, spread sweetly open in the splaying of her legs.

"Tell me, sweetheart," he said. "What do you understand?" He took a wipe from the package and warmed it in his hands. Darla's eyes widened as she saw what he was doing, as if she hadn't realized he would have to wipe her diaper area before he put more powder on and put her into her fresh diaper.

"I understand… oh, daddy, that tickles!"

"Does it tickle?" Mike said, swabbing up and down a little teasingly. "Or does it make you feel naughty again?"

"Both, daddy," Darla giggled. "Oh…"

Mike had started to rub the wipe firmly around her anus. "What did you understand, Darla?" he asked. He resisted the temptation to insert a finger in her tiny rose, just to make her squeal.

"Um…" Finally Mike finished the wiping, putting the little towel in the pail. He got the powder. Darla looked a little disappointed that the wiping had finished. "I understand that the diapers are to teach me that the things I do need to show that I'm a grownup, and I can take responsibility for what I did."

Mike smiled. "That's a good way to put it, sweetheart. Can you say more? How does it relate to how you got here, as daddy's little girl, when you're much too old for diapers and spankings?" He took the fresh diaper gently from Darla's hands, marveling again at the tiny perfections of her breasts with their little brown nipples.

"When I stole that stuff, I wasn't acting like a grownup," Darla said simply. "I wasn't thinking about right and wrong, or who I might hurt by taking stuff from the store."

Mike fastened the fresh diaper over her hips. "I'm

proud of you, Darla," he said. His diaper girl smiled up at him. "Let's get you into your nightgown and snuggle you up for a few minutes before dinner. After dinner you'll go right to bed."

Mike stood and went to the dresser.

"Can I sit up, daddy?" Darla asked.

"Yes, sweetheart," he said, getting the nightgown out of the drawer. "Put your hands over your head and daddy will put your nighty on for you."

So she did, stretching her fingers toward the ceiling and looking at Mike with a curious expression, as if confused at how he could move from discipline to care to sex so rapidly.

*Well*, Mike thought, *that makes two of us.*

# CHAPTER NINE

After dinner, during which Darla tried to forget that she had a diaper on and mostly succeeded as Mike taught her to make a simple red sauce, something she had always supposed was possible but never witnessed in the real world, she put the dishes in the dishwasher and padded off to brush her teeth and get into bed to wait for her story. She knew she would have to have another change before she went to sleep, but she didn't want to think about it; she felt strangely content to be in the little pink bed in the little pink room, going to bed early, with her daddy on the way to tell her a story.

Then, though, as she listened through her door to Mike going about his own evening routine (Darla wondered what it held—she had never lived with a man since she had left home at fourteen, and before that she had never thought to pay much attention) she realized that her hand had drifted down, inside her nightgown, just to feel the thick cotton of the diaper. Not to try to touch her pussy, because she knew she would get a spanking if Mike caught her doing that, but just to know what it felt like to be an eighteen-year-old girl who had to wear a diaper, and had to pee in it, because she needed to learn a lesson.

Yes, of course, Darla knew what it felt like, she supposed, because apparently she *was* that eighteen-year-old in a diaper, but the sensation of the fabric, and transition from its thickness, so different from grownup panties, to the skin of her thighs, of her tummy… it made her feel funny. Embarrassed, ashamed, but also somehow… happy. Just testing, she moved her fingers down, to see if she could feel them at all through the diaper, on the place her daddy had shaved because Darla had lost the privilege of having her hair there.

She could feel them, but only very vaguely, and rather frustratingly, as if her diaper, as well as demonstrating her need for discipline, also ensured that Darla not experience naughty big-girl pleasures between her thighs. If she put her hand inside… but daddy would spank her…

Darla gave a little whimper of frustration as she tried desperately to decide whether she wanted to risk putting her hand inside her diaper, to touch the pussy that she could feel becoming so warm and wet. Would she need to be changed not because she'd peed but because she couldn't control her naughty-girl urges? She rubbed the diaper harder, bit her lip, moaned softly.

The door opened. "What are you doing, sweetheart?" Mike said, apparently noting her splayed position, though she had only touched the diaper under the covers and her daddy really couldn't see, could he?

She snatched her hand away, trying to move it in such a way as to look like she was scratching her tummy. "Nothing, daddy." Darla's voice sounded guilty to her ears, but how could you ever say things like *Nothing, daddy* without sounding guilty?

"It didn't look like nothing, sweetheart," Mike said very seriously.

"Oh, daddy," Darla said. "I was just… I didn't have my hand inside! I swear it! I just wanted to feel what it felt like on the outside!"

Mike had come into the room and he stood now

looming over Darla where she lay on the little bed. She looked up into his face, hoping that he would see that she had told the truth—or pretty close to it, at least.

"I can see," her daddy said slowly, "that you're being honest about not touching yourself inside your diaper. That's good. But I'm not sure you're telling me the whole truth."

Darla felt a crinkle trouble her brow. How did he know that? Did he have some magical daddy superpower? Her mouth shaped itself into the pout that seemed to occupy it so often these days, in her daddy's house.

"Don't make your boo-boo face, Darla," Mike said sharply. "You need to tell me the truth."

"My what?" What was that supposed to mean, *boo-boo face*? Then she remembered about addressing him properly, and added, "Daddy, what do you mean?"

"That little pout. I call it a boo-boo face. When I see you make it, I know I need to treat you like a little girl."

"You mean, spank me, daddy?" Darla whispered. "Spank my bare bottom?" Why had she said that?

But maybe it had been the right thing to say, because she saw a little smile break out on Mike's face, then. "Sometimes it means you need a spanking," he said. "But sometimes it means you need a hug, and sometimes it means you need a treat."

"Sometimes all three?" Darla whispered, feeling herself go red but not knowing how to stop. "And the treat with daddy's beautiful cock?"

Mike gave that little headshake that seemed to mean he couldn't get over the things his little girl said sometimes, but then he nodded slowly. "That's right, sweetheart. Sometimes the treat should be something only big girls are allowed to do, and only daddies can give them, with a hard cock in their private places. So stop making the boo-boo face and tell me what you were doing. I told you that if you're a good girl tonight and tomorrow, you'll have a treat coming."

"With daddy's cock?" The eagerness in her own voice took Darla aback, made the flush in her cheeks even hotter.

"We'll see, sweetheart," Mike said.

*We'll see!* That meant yes, didn't it? Suddenly a vision of herself, riding up and down on the big, hard cock she had had to suck just a couple hours before, crying out that her daddy was too big for her little pussy, filled her mind and nearly robbed her of her senses. She swallowed hard, then had to clear her throat.

Mike clearly noticed that something had disturbed his little girl's peace of mind. "What is it, sweetheart?" he asked with concern.

Darla's cheeks burned even more. "It's something very naughty, daddy," she whispered. "I can't say…" But she *wanted* to say, she realized suddenly, even if her daddy would spank her for it. *Especially* if he would spank her for it. She dropped her voice even lower and spoke rapidly, lowering her eyes and not daring to look at Mike. "It's just that I was thinking about what it will be like when my daddy fucks me."

"Language, Darla," Mike said sharply. "That's quite enough of that. You just earned yourself a spanking. Get out from the covers and kneel on your bed, then bend over on your elbows and present your bottom for punishment."

She felt the boo-boo face re-emerge. "I'm sorry, daddy," she said. "Did I… did I ruin my treat, for tomorrow?"

"No, you didn't ruin the treat, if you take your spanking like a good girl now. This is a separate matter, but I can't let it pass."

"Over my diaper?" Darla said hopefully.

"Of course not, young lady. I'll be taking your diaper down as soon as you get into position. And you'd better do that right now, if you don't want the belt."

Darla gave a startled little cry. She didn't think she was

as scared of anything—even of the *special lessons* whose nature she still didn't fathom—as she was of her daddy's belt. She scrambled out from under the covers and onto her elbows, realizing as she did so that the position would be perfect for… well, for fucking. She tried to raise her bottom high, arching her back as she felt her cheeks flush pink again at the terrible indignity of having to present herself that way.

"Good girl," Mike said. Darla felt his hands brushing against her thighs as he rolled up her nightgown to expose the diaper. She expected him to undo the Velcro immediately, but instead, to Darla's distress, he began to stroke her bottom through the flannel, running his hand down to her bare thighs and then back up again, to cup her whole little bottom in its shameful white covering. "Before I take down this diaper, sweetheart, I want you to finish telling me what you were about to tell me before you went off on your naughty little fantasy about daddy's cock. You were going to tell me the truth about what you were doing with your hand when I came in."

Her daddy's hand was there now, moving down, rubbing firmly between Darla's thighs, and the muffled sensation of the thick cotton moving against her bare pussy, much more roughly than she had done with her own fingers, made her give a little cry of mingled pleasure and surprise.

"Please, daddy!" she said. "I want to be good! That makes me feel so funny!"

"You'll feel funny when your daddy thinks you should feel funny, Darla. Is this what you were doing, touching yourself through your diaper?"

"Yes, daddy," Darla whispered. "I only wanted to feel how different it was to have to wear a diaper instead of my big-girl panties. And it made me think about… about you, and… and what you have for me. You know, the… ah… oh, daddy… the, um, thing between your legs that gets so… hard. To, um, to put… to p-put in between my legs,

and wherever you want to put it, because daddies g-get to s-say… and… and naughty little girls have to do as they're told."

Mike kept rubbing her pussy through the diaper as she spoke, so that she was sure he would see how wet she had gotten when he opened it up. That thought even made her try to ride his hand a little, seeking some pleasure even though the thick fabric made it so faint. Little whimpers came from her throat, into the silence that had fallen. What would her daddy say?

Finally, stilling his hand but leaving it possessively on her bottom, he said, "Thank you for telling me the truth, sweetheart. I think I understand."

Then, without another word, he reached his hands to the fasteners of the diaper and pulled them open. The diaper dropped to the bed, and Darla's face got very hot once again as she imagined the way she looked to her daddy: innocent, because he had shaved her pussy and taken away the grownup hair, but terribly wicked, too, because he must be able to see just how wet she had gotten, thinking about her daddy fucking her.

Suddenly he had put his left arm around her waist. She felt the soft cotton of his black T-shirt come up against her left hip as he wrapped his bare forearm around her tummy to hold her fast.

"Daddy?" she said, questioning, not understanding, but then Mike started to spank her, hard and quick, making sure he could punish exactly the place on Darla's backside that he wanted to punish by holding her very tightly with his other arm.

"Ow! Daddy! Please! It hurts so much!" Her daddy had decided to spank her even harder tonight than he had the first time, yesterday, and he was spanking quickly and steadily, in the same place over and over until it blazed like fire and made her tears come trickling down onto the bed, before he moved to the next spot.

"Of course it hurts, Darla," Mike said grimly. "You

need to learn that you'll get what you deserve, no matter how much your daddy wants to gratify those naughty desires of yours."

He kept spanking, and now Darla began to scream, because her bottom felt like it would never be the same, so hard did her daddy spank it. She struggled, because she couldn't help it, but Mike hardly let her move an inch, and kept spanking until she went limp, sobbing, in his grasp.

"That doesn't feel as good as touching yourself, does it now, Darla?" Mike asked in a softer tone.

"No, daddy," she sobbed.

"When daddy is punishing you by making you wear a diaper, to teach you to obey him and follow his rules, you mustn't confuse your punishment with pleasure, and you mustn't try to distract daddy by using lewd language and talking about lewd things. I think I may have been wrong to let you suck daddy's cock, but now that you have, daddy needs to keep your big-girl urges under his control. That's why I had to spank you so hard. Do you think you understand?"

"Yes, daddy," Darla sniffled.

"Alright," Mike said. "I'm going to fasten your diaper back up, and then you'll wet it. I'll change you again, and then we can have a bedtime story, okay?"

"Okay, daddy."

# CHAPTER TEN

When Darla lay under the covers again, looking adorably up at him, her eyes still bright with tears at the terrible punishment Mike had had to give her, Mike sat at the end of her bed and said, "Once upon a time there was a princess who was naughty and got spanked."

"Did her daddy put her in a diaper, just like me?"

"Yes, he did." He thought for a moment, then couldn't resist saying, "She was eighteen, and actually her daddy wasn't related to her."

"Oh," said Darla thoughtfully. "Maybe she came from another kingdom, and was staying at her daddy's castle as his ward."

Mike felt a grin break out on his face. "Yes, that's it. You're sharp as a tack, aren't you, sweetheart?"

"Thanks, daddy," Darla said, smiling up brightly at him. "So if she was eighteen…" Her eyes seemed desperate, but Mike could tell that she had learned her lesson about introducing forbidden topics.

"Her daddy the king could do big-girl things with her," Mike nodded.

"Like what, daddy?" Darla asked.

"Well, when she was good, the king would unfasten the

princess' diaper sometimes and look at her there, and tell her how pretty she looked between her legs."

"Oh," was all Darla could say, apparently.

"Then he would talk to her about how important it was to keep herself clean, and not to touch herself unless she had permission."

Darla nodded. "Because she had to be a good girl, and wait until the right prince came along to give her permission, and teach her how to please him."

Mike chuckled at the solemn look in her eyes. For a moment he struggled with his desire for her, and his desire to reward her for her penitence and her good behavior as his diaper girl. Should he not give her any treat tonight?

But she showed so much understanding and acceptance of his authority that he thought a positive reinforcement might well help. As he reached out for the comforter, he looked into Darla's eyes so that he saw the wonder in them as he gently pulled it down with the sheet, then tugged her nightgown up over her hips to expose the diaper.

"Was it like this?" Darla asked. "When the king looked at the princess?"

"Yes, sweetheart. Lie on your back, now, and spread your knees nice and wide." Mike opened the fresh diaper he had changed her into just a few minutes before, and pulled the front down. "Your pussy is just as pretty as the princess' was, Darla," he said softly. "Neat and tidy, and very demure."

"Did the... did the king ever..."

But Mike was already reaching down with his right hand, and he laid his hand gently there, loving the feeling of his little girl's bare pussy. He moved two fingers up and down lightly, and Darla's words trailed off into a moan. She closed her eyes, her forehead creased with an adorable, pleasure-driven version of the boo-boo face.

"Oh, daddy," she sighed. "What did the king say?"

"The king said that if the princess could learn to be

good, and she earned the right to wear big-girl underwear, the king would teach her how to please a man, and how much pleasure a man can give a princess." Up and down, up and down, with his fingers—then inward, just a little, and back up, with a delicious slippery motion that made Mike's cock so hard that he knew he wouldn't be able to wait long to have his little girl under him as he thrust in and out of the pussy he had bared. Not tonight, though.

Darla cried out as he rubbed her clit more and more firmly now. Mike said, "The king told the princess that it was natural for her to have big-girl feelings, now that she was eighteen, and that when he touched her, she should let those feelings out, until they got so strong that they made her melt away. He said that was called *coming*. I'm going to make you come now, sweetheart."

Her only response came in the little cries she made, her eyes still firmly shut and her cheeks very pink. Mike watched the naughty big-girl things his fingers did, enraptured, feeling her pussy flutter around the fingers he moved in and out faster and faster.

"Come for me, princess," he said softly. "Come right now, because your daddy says so."

Darla's hands had lain clasped at her chest as Mike pulled down the covers and raised her nightgown and opened her diaper. Now, suddenly, Mike felt her clutch his denim-covered thigh with her right hand as she threw her left above her head in a tiny fist. He looked at her, a little surprised by the intensity of the grip on his thigh, and he saw that she had opened her eyes, to look down her body with an expression on her face almost of distress, as if she couldn't bear to see that her daddy's hand was there between her legs, but she couldn't bear not to see it either.

Then, with a cry of ecstasy, her head went back, her eyes closed once again, and every muscle in her little body seemed to go tense, her hips bucking lewdly against her daddy's hand. Mike kept moving his fingers in and out of her adorable pink pussy until her moans had subsided to

little whimpers.

"Thank you, daddy," Darla whispered. "Did the king do anything else with the princess?"

"Not that night," Mike said, smiling down at her as he closed her diaper back up.

"What about the next night, daddy?" Her voice sounded wonderfully sleepy all of a sudden.

"The next night, the king fucked the princess," Mike said very softly.

"Daddy! You shouldn't say things like that!"

"Daddies can talk any way they want, sweetheart."

Darla's brow creased. "Yes, daddy. But I'm not allowed to say that?"

"No, you're not. Just like you're not allowed to decide when your daddy puts his cock in you."

She bit her lip at that, then gave a little nod. "Okay, daddy." She seemed to be working her courage up to say something, then.

"What is it, sweetheart?" Mike asked.

"Can I have a goodnight kiss, daddy?" Darla blurted out quickly.

Mike smiled. "Of course, sweetheart," he said.

"On my lips?"

Mike responded by bending down and giving Darla a big-girl kiss to take her breath away, fondling her little breasts at the same time.

"Oh, daddy," she said when he pulled away. "Are you sure the king didn't… you know… that same night?"

"Yes, sweetheart," Mike said, maintaining his paternal tone despite the hardness of his cock. "I'm sure. You be a good girl for me tomorrow in your diaper, and we'll see how the bedtime story goes."

• • • • • • •

When he knocked on her door and poked his head into her room the next morning, he found Darla awake. He

could see on her face that realizing she had a diaper on under her nightgown had made for a strange sort of awakening.

He watched her look at the clock and see that the early bedtime Mike enforced made it possible to wake up even before he came to make sure. Then he thought he could see in her dark eyes that the memories of the previous evening had come flooding back.

Then, to his delight, he saw the blood rush to her face as she said, "I'm awake, daddy."

"Do you need a change?" Mike asked matter-of-factly. Even in the dim morning light he could see that her blush increased at that.

"Not yet, daddy," she said.

"Well, hurry up and do your business, and I'll change you. Go ahead. Right now."

"Oh, daddy, can't I go to the bathroom this morning?"

"No, Darla. Of course you can't. You're a diaper girl until I say otherwise."

"But I don't *have* to go right now," she pleaded.

"Don't lie to me, sweetheart. I know how little girls' bodies work. You didn't have this trouble last night when you were sucking daddy's cock, did you?"

At that, her blush returned in full force. "No, daddy."

"Should daddy put his cock in your mouth, to help you?"

The little crinkle appeared on her brow. She gave a cute little nod. Mike certainly hadn't planned on this kind of thing this morning, but they did have time before she needed to get to work, and having his diaper girl at his disposal seemed to put his cock in a constant state of erection. He had no objection at all to putting his morning wood in his naughty little girl's velvety mouth and starting her day with a nice helping of daddy's seed.

He stepped to the side of her bed, and lowered his green flannel pajama bottoms so that his cock sprang free to hang a few inches above Darla's face. "Pull down the

# CHAPTER ELEVEN

Darla could hardly concentrate on work at all that day. Joanne had discovered more facts about the new correctional programs delivered by Selecta and its competitors, and she wouldn't let the matter go, so as customers came and went for their oil changes and brake jobs, Darla found herself treated involuntarily to lurid tales that mirrored her own situation in Mike's house much too closely.

"This one girl, she said on her blog, she had to be naked in her correctional officer's house all the time, and when she met a guy he had to talk to the officer, and the officer told him that the girl was under his supervision, and if they had sex the guy had to do it in his house, and the guy had to, you know, dominate her. Really weird." Joanne was scrolling through a long series of parts orders, so she couldn't see Darla blush, thank goodness. Darla's diaper felt bunchy and strange under her skirt. She kept having to remember to cross her legs to make sure Joanne didn't notice anything weird, and when she did, the diaper's thickness felt even stranger.

"What does that mean?" Darla asked, trying to keep her tone completely neutral.

"Well," Joanne said doubtfully, lowering her voice. "I don't know if you're into this kind of thing, but I had a boyfriend—a guy named Joe—a couple of years ago…" Joanne was in her late twenties, and, from her own account, pretty sexually experienced. She dropped her volume even further. "He liked to tie me up, you know, and then, you know, do it like that."

She giggled. Darla looked intently at her own computer screen, trying to focus on the oil-change receipt she was processing despite the heat in her cheeks.

"And, you know," Joanne continued, "other stuff, too."

"Like what?" Darla couldn't keep herself from asking. The *special lessons* her daddy might teach her, the ones she still didn't understand, loomed large in her mind.

"Like spanking, and toys, and things. Lots of stuff. He said he liked to show me who was the boss in the bedroom, and he made rules for me, and if I broke them, he put me over his knee and spanked me. I don't know about you, but I think that's kind of hot."

Which must be why Joanne had become obsessed with these correctional programs. Darla breathed a little sigh of relief; she had worried that Joanne had somehow known that Darla herself had been put into the custody of Selecta.

"Maybe," Darla said. Then, to her surprise, she found herself wanting to continue the conversation. "But I think even if it's something people do for fun, it's probably pretty effective as a way of getting women who have committed crimes to understand the need for discipline, don't you think?"

She risked a glance at Joanne, who had turned to her with an appraising expression. "Yes," the older woman admitted. "I guess that's right. When Joe spanked me, I kind of felt like he really was teaching me a lesson. And that's what the girl said on her blog, too. The correctional officer gave the new boyfriend a paddle, and made him spank the girl with it while he watched to make sure the

guy did it right. Then he told the guy to take her to her room and have sex with her—she says she had to ask her correctional officer if she could please have sex, and she had to promise that she would submit to the new boyfriend."

"Then what happened?" Darla breathed. She realized suddenly that her bladder's fullness, after three cups of coffee, had snuck up on her. The strange conversation with Joanne seemed to have encouraged it, and now the images of this nameless other girl, in a correctional program like Darla's own, though apparently without the regression to little-girlhood and the diapers, submitting to a fucking by her new boyfriend, on the instructions of a correctional officer like Darla's own strict daddy, seemed to push Darla's own feelings about her discipline into a new realm.

In that new realm, to pee in her diaper right here and now, at her workstation, while Joanne told her the story of the nameless girl's fucking, seemed like the kind of thing Darla might do, to show that she had begun to understand what her daddy was trying to teach her.

"You really want to hear this?" Joanne asked.

Darla kept her eyes focused on her screen. "Uh-huh," she said. "It's kind of hot, right?" *Flat tone. Keep the flat tone.*

"Yeah, super-hot," Joanne agreed. "I just didn't know if you were into it. But you seem a little different this week, Darla. I've been trying to talk to you about this stuff for months. I want us to be, you know, girlfriends who talk about sex and stuff."

Was that true? With a strange sense of recognition Darla realized that it was. Whenever Joanne had brought up anything racy, which—Dara remembered now—often included references to things like toys and rope and guys Joanne said she would give blowjobs at a moment's notice, Darla had pretended she hadn't heard. Now that her criminal record had brought her into her daddy's custody, it all seemed much more relevant.

She shifted awkwardly in her seat; not only was her bladder almost becoming painful, but it seemed to reinforce the arousal Joanne's account of the nameless girl had begun to evoke in her diaper-covered pussy. Shouldn't she just excuse herself and go to the bathroom to wet her diaper?

"I guess I just finally caught on," she said lamely.

"Well, it's about time!" Joanne said, giggling. "Now we'll have to find you a guy who can spank you."

Darla couldn't help it. She looked at Joanne with an expression that she knew would tell the older woman everything, or close to it.

"You already have!" Joanne said in a whisper. "Spill! All about him! How old is he? Where does he live?"

Darla shook her head. The new realm seemed to take over, surround her. "I'm in one of those programs," she whispered back. Then, hardly believing she was doing it, she took a deep breath, turned her swivel chair to face Joanne, and uncrossed her legs.

Joanne gave her a puzzled expression, but then she clearly saw the anxious look on Darla's face. "Tell me," she said gently.

Darla showed her instead. She reached down to her knees and raised her skirt, gathering it to her waist, so that Joanne could see her diaper. "I have to wet my diaper," she said. "Then I have to call my daddy to come change me."

Then, overcome by the sheer submissiveness of the moment, she started to pee, right there in the cashier's office of the car dealership, while Joanne watched, wide-eyed. Darla closed her eyes because although something about having her coworker watch her as she did the shameful thing seemed so terribly arousing that she couldn't have stopped herself if she tried, she also couldn't bear to see the horror that part of her knew would appear on Joanne's face.

At last she finished, and she opened her eyes and

looked at Joanne, who checked nervously to make sure no customers were approaching the counter, then looked back at Darla and visibly swallowed hard. "So you're in one of the… little girl programs?" she ventured softly.

Darla nodded. "Daddy's Naughty Little Girl," she said, with a grimace.

"What did you do?"

"Shoplifting," Darla admitted, "but, you know, more than once." Realizing that she was still showing Joanne her diaper, now with a horribly embarrassing faint yellow stain on the front, she lowered her skirt again self-consciously.

"Does it… I mean, is it… working?" Joanne's brow furrowed, as if she were trying to keep herself from saying something, but then she said, "Does your daddy spank you?"

"Yes," Darla whispered. "Twice so far. He's pretty strict with me. But…" She felt her blush return. "He's really nice, too. He makes me feel safe, and like I don't want to break the law again. I want to, you know, be a good girl for him."

"Is he cute?" Joanne's own cheeks turned a little pink as she asked the question, Darla noticed.

"Well… yeah. I mean… he's older, you know, and I never thought I'd be into that…" Darla's mind turned again to the question of *special lessons*, and together with the terribly naughty damp feeling in her wet diaper that made her whole body seem to quiver with shame.

"But you are?" Joanne asked, though her tone made it only half a question, if that.

Darla nodded. "I need to text him so he'll come change me," she whispered.

"Here? In the dealership?"

"In the car." Darla couldn't even look at Joanne, then, so she fumbled for her phone in her purse instead.

"Does he do… I mean, you know…"

"What?" Darla asked distractedly, not catching on to what Joanne might be curious about.

Joanne wheeled her chair closer and leaned in, whispering, "Sex stuff. They can do that, right? As long as they don't, you know, put it in?"

If Darla thought she had blushed hotly before— whether in the last ten minutes or in her entire life to that point—she realized now that she had been wrong. She thought for a moment that her face would melt. She couldn't keep from picturing her daddy's cock, the way it had looked and the way it had tasted when he had made her suck it—which was how she thought of it, even though Darla herself had been the one so desperate for it, and the one who asked to suck Mike's penis.

"I'm just gonna text him, okay?"

"Oh, my God," Joanne breathed. "He has, hasn't he? Just like that girl on the blog!"

Darla didn't think she could have found anything to say to that even if she had wanted to answer.

She texted.

*Hi daddy; I'm ready for a change.*

She kept staring down at the phone, willing Mike to text back instantly so that she wouldn't have to keep talking to Joanne. Darla liked feeling that she had a friend to talk to about the very strange things that seemed to be happening to her and inside her, but right now it just felt too embarrassing.

"The girl on the blog said that her officer made her wear a plug in her ass," Joanne blurted out. "Do you have to do that?"

At least the question had a concrete element to it, so Darla felt like she could respond. "No," she said. "But it sounds like that's a different kind of program, right? Did she have to wear a diaper?"

"No," Joanne admitted.

Darla almost asked, *Did her officer shave her between her legs?*, but thank goodness the text came back from Mike at

that moment.

*Wait outside. There in two minutes.*

"I have to go," Darla said, trying not to let the relief become too obvious in her voice. She didn't want to offend Joanne because the older woman really seemed to have taken the idea that she had a criminal who had to wear a diaper as a coworker in stride, but the fascination Joanne manifested made Darla feel funny, and—though she would never admit it to Joanne and didn't even want to admit it to herself—almost painfully aroused.

She hadn't really had to walk in a wet diaper before, let alone do it in public. She felt certain that as she moved through the showroom of the dealership someone would notice that her face seemed to have turned an alarming shade of scarlet, but she made it out the door to see her daddy leaning against his car, and her heart gave a little leap.

She ran to him, both simply wanting to get it over with and because to her surprise she felt very happy to see him. Mike opened his arms to her and gave her a hug, and that surprised her too. "Good girl," he said. "We'll get you changed nice and quick."

Darla's daddy changed her diaper in the back of his truck. Darla knew his muscular form hid her from view, but the shame of having that done in public, as if she were a two-year-old who had had an accident, seemed to drive her to new depths of mortification. She closed her eyes as Mike put the lotion on, knowing she was making her boo-boo face for him because of the pleasure she couldn't help feeling even though Mike didn't seem interested in stimulating her, really.

"Daddy?" she asked as he closed the fresh diaper up at last over her hips.

"Yes, sweetheart?" he asked.

"What's a special lesson?"

"You'll find out tonight, Darla," Mike said. "I promise."

# CHAPTER TWELVE

After driving her home from work, Mike took Darla out of diapers at last, and watched her pee on the toilet like a big girl. The sight of the golden stream emerging from her bare, pink pussy aroused him so much that he couldn't wait.

When she had dried herself, he said, "No panties yet, sweetheart. Daddy's going to fuck you right now. Go to daddy's room and take off all your clothes and lie on daddy's bed with your legs up, just like you're going to have your diaper changed. After daddy fucks your pussy, you'll get dressed in your pinafore with your big-girl panties underneath. Then we'll have dinner. You'll have your reward and your special lesson at bedtime."

Darla stared at him wide-eyed for a moment. Then she said very quietly, "Yes, daddy." She stood still, though, as if she were trying to figure out whether she should obey him, or wait to see what would happen if she didn't.

"Do you want daddy to fuck your little pussy, sweetheart?" he asked gently, though he could see the answer in her face.

"Yes, daddy," she whispered. She had let the hem of the little blue dress she had worn to work fall to her knees

again.

"Lift your skirt again, and show daddy where you want him to put his cock." That cock had grown so incredibly hard at the thought of fucking Darla that Mike began to contemplate having her here in the bathroom, bent over the sink. *Not this time*, he thought. *Something more traditional this time.*

As if in a trance, Darla moved her hands to the front of the little dress and pulled it up to her waist, so that her sweet little pussy, bare and pink and pouting, appeared before her daddy's eyes again. Mike took a step forward and put his own hand down, and grasped his little girl there very gently, rubbing only a very, very little, so that Darla gave a tiny whimper. The silky feeling there, and the knowledge that he would soon be inside her, experiencing the lovely tightness of his eighteen-year-old naughty girl, made his cock give a little leap in his pants.

"Tell me, then, Darla. Tell me what you want your daddy to do."

He looked down into her dark eyes. The expression on her face seemed to mingle anxiety, arousal, and mischief, all in equal measure. Mike found her so bewitching he could hardly believe he had had the luck to be appointed to guide her to true maturity. *God bless our corporate overlords*, he thought with an inward chuckle.

"I want my daddy to fuck my little pussy with his big, hard cock," she whispered all in a rush and then bit her lip as she looked up at him. "You won't spank me for saying that, will you, daddy? Please? You told me to say it!"

"No, I won't spank you now, sweetheart," Mike said, moving his middle finger softly against her clit so that Darla shuddered and her nostrils flared with the arousal he forced upon her. "As long as you do as I've said, and go to my bedroom to get ready for fucking."

"Oh, God," Darla moaned, obviously just as aroused by her daddy's wicked words as by his wicked touch. "I will, daddy. I want to please you so much."

Mike bent down and gave her a long, passionate kiss, using his tongue to tell her that her daddy would have his way with her, just as he liked. A little reluctantly, then, he relinquished his hold on the soft, wet place between his little girl's thighs, and stepped back to take a last look at her obediently holding her skirt up to show him where he would take his pleasure in his bed.

"Should I go now, daddy?" she asked.

"Yes, sweetheart, but hold your skirt up as you walk, to remind you that daddy gets to look at your pussy whenever he wants, and fuck it whenever he wants, now, too."

She gave one of her cute little nods, and, still looking at his face as she left the bathroom, until she had passed by him into the hall, she did at last obey. Mike watched her pass by her own door, her skirt still held high, and then go into his room, where she had never been before.

*She'll spend a lot of time in my bed from now on*, he promised himself. Mike had always enjoyed sex greatly, and he had always fucked girls dominantly, but his relationship with Darla seemed to have kicked his dominance up a notch. He wasn't sure he could ever get enough of the feeling of benevolent control he got from having the power to enjoy his sweet girl just as he liked, knowing that every time he exercised his paternal authority over her, it helped guide her to feel more in charge of herself.

He followed her down the hall to his room, and found her in bed just as he had specified, holding her knees up and apart so that he found himself greeted delightfully by the sweet pink pout of the pussy he would now claim as his own. She had closed her eyes, as if the scene were too shameful to look at, or perhaps she wanted to turn herself over to him completely.

"Darla, look at me," Mike said softly.

She had her head on the pillow, so when her dark eyes flew open she could confront his gaze, looking between her thighs and over her bare pussy to where Mike now stood at the end of the bed.

"I want you to watch daddy get undressed. I want you to take a good look at how hard you get daddy's cock. You're a sweet little naughty girl who needs fucking because you got your daddy so hard."

"Are you... are you going to spank me? Because I got your cock so hard, daddy?" Darla asked in a dreamy voice that puzzled Mike for a moment. Just for a moment, though, because then he thought he understood.

"Should I spank you for that, sweetheart?" he asked. He had pulled off his T-shirt, and now he began to unbuckle his belt. "Should I whip you with this belt, maybe?" He pulled the belt free from his waist, and doubled it in his hands, holding it up for Darla to see. Her eyes widened.

"If you think I need it, daddy," she said in a fearful whisper that nevertheless made Mike feel certain she had felt her pussy respond to the sight of the belt, ready to teach her a stern lesson about modesty, and what naughty little girls have coming. "Do you think I need it?"

"I think I should give you a little taste of the belt, Darla," Mike said. "So you understand how serious a thing it is, when you get your daddy hard."

"Yes, daddy," she said. "I know. Your cock is very important, isn't it?"

Mike almost laughed at that, but she had said it with such a straight face that he found himself continuing on in the same vein. "Yes, sweetheart," he said. "That's right."

"Can I see it? While you whip me with your belt?"

"No, Darla. You'll see it when I'm ready to fuck you."

"Daddy gets to say," she whispered, as if to herself.

He looked down at her, so sweetly ready for him, her pink inner lips peeping out between the pale outer ones, all bare and smooth. "That's right, sweetheart. Now close your knees and keep holding them up. Daddy's going to whip you in that position."

Darla nodded and obeyed. To Mike's delight, he saw that her pussy remained just visible between her thighs. He

reached out with his left arm and wrapped it around those thighs, taking hold of them and pulling her down the bed as she gave a little cry of surprise. He let go of Darla for just long enough to wind the doubled belt once around his fist, and then seized her firmly once again and began to whip his little girl's bottom—not very hard, rather just to make her feel disciplined, as he knew she needed.

"Oh, daddy," she said in a whimper. "Oh, please…"

"Please what, sweetheart?" Mike asked, as he kept giving her sharp little lashes with the belt that rang out in the bedroom with a slapping sound that satisfied him greatly.

"I want my treat so much, daddy," she said. "If I don't get it right now I think I'm gonna die!"

"Is your pussy having big-girl feelings?" Mike asked sternly. He brought the belt down a little harder, as if to punish her for her arousal.

"Yes, daddy. Is that naughty? I just want your cock inside me so much! And that's making me want my treat worse than I ever wanted to touch myself before. When you whip me I feel like I'm learning my lesson, and that makes me want to show you my pussy and touch it while you watch, to make your cock nice and hard so that my daddy can have his way and use my body to make himself feel good."

Mike felt his eyes widen at Darla's rather amazing declaration. "That *is* naughty, but it also makes you a good girl, too, because you confessed, and you asked permission. I'm going to hold your legs open now and watch you play with yourself, until you have a nice big orgasm, okay? You've earned it by learning to wet your diaper when daddy says so, and by sucking daddy's cock so well."

He let go of her thighs with his left arm and straightened up, taking hold of her knees, right hand still holding the belt as well, and spread them. Again he met Darla's eyes over the adorable sight of her glistening pussy,

"Are you coming, sweetheart?" he asked softly.

"Yes, daddy," Darla cried, then simply kept saying it, "yes, daddy… yes, daddy…" until her words were lost in the bucking of her hips and her long cry of climax.

# CHAPTER THIRTEEN

Darla's handsome daddy let go of her knees. With a little sob, she moved her hands away from her pussy, and back up her thighs. She knew she needed to keep herself open, because her daddy liked to look at the pussy he had shaved; the place where his little girl had to give him his way, the place where she needed his hardness, his authority, so very badly now.

As he swiftly drew his jeans and briefs down, Mike seemed to keep looking at that pussy, and, she felt sure, at the wicked place where he had made her put her finger. Darla often ran her hands over her bottom, and even touched herself on her bottom-hole, when she played with herself, but to have to put her finger inside was new, and it had been very embarrassing to watch Mike's eyes fixed downward on the shameful act. And her daddy had said he would put his big, hard penis there, too!

He held his cock in his left hand, now, rubbing it gently. Darla wondered for a moment why the thing that was so naughty for little girls was just fine for daddies, but of course she knew the answer: daddies get to say. If a daddy liked to stroke his hard cock before he put it in his little girl's pussy, he got to do that.

"Spread that pussy open for me, Darla," he said then, looking up into her eyes for the first time since she had had her treat. "Show me where daddy's cock goes."

The position felt terribly uncomfortable and terribly arousing at once, pulling her now-aching legs back and putting her fingertips where she could spread herself open like the naughtiest girl in the world. Mike stepped forward, and Darla sobbed with pleasure simply at the way he took the weight of her legs on his chest, and gripped her left hip with his right hand so he could put the head of his cock right in the warm, pink place Darla showed him.

She looked up at him, blushed as she saw that her daddy's gaze was focused downward at how his big cock had started to enter his little girl's inexperienced pussy. Then, though, just as she felt him begin to rush inside her, he lifted his eyes and met her gaze with a smile of pleasure that nearly took her breath away.

"Oh, it's a nice pussy," he said. "Such a nice pussy for daddy to fuck."

"It feels good, daddy?" Darla asked timidly.

"Yes, sweetheart. Very good. You're nice and tight, just the way daddy likes it. Daddy's going to fuck very hard now, so don't be frightened, okay?"

"I won't be, daddy. It feels nice for me, too. I like having a cock inside me, like a big girl."

Mike gave a little grunt of pleasure at that, as if at the filthiness of Darla's words as much as the tightness of her pussy. Darla smiled, giggled a little, even, despite the wickedness, as her daddy fulfilled his promise and began to move in and out hard and fast, his cock surging into her so far that it took Darla's breath away.

"Do you like that?" he asked, a little breathlessly. "Do you like getting what you deserve, you naughty girl?"

"It feels so good, daddy!" Darla cried. "Thank you, daddy! I… I love your big cock…" Now that Mike had called her naughty, it seemed like she couldn't seem to stop talking dirty. "It's what bad girls get, isn't it? Big, hard

cocks in their pussies, and their bottoms, to teach them to behave?"

She looked up at him, looked down at where his penis rushed in and out of her bare little vagina. She gasped at the sheer lewdness of the sight, looked up again to find her daddy looking down into her eyes with an expression of dominant pleasure that took her breath away again.

"That's right, sweetheart. In this house bad girls get fucked hard, the way they deserve."

"Oh, daddy," she moaned. "I'm going to come again."

"Go ahead and come, sweetheart. Come on daddy's cock. Daddy will come inside you in a moment because your pussy feels so good. See if you can come when daddy does."

Then, looking down at the place where he had joined his body to Darla's, he moved both his hands to her shoulders, not around her neck but right next to it so that Darla shivered and started to come just at the feeling of being controlled that way. Mike had started to pound her bottom—tingly from the light belt-whipping—very hard. As if at the feeling of her pussy contracting around his cock with her orgasm, though, he went still, every muscle in his powerful body seeming to tense for a long moment and his face looking terribly dominant to Darla.

Her daddy's hips spasmed hard against her bottom, then, and she felt his seed start to spurt inside her. Now suddenly she couldn't stop coming and she writhed in his grip, her inability to twist free of his hands, his hips, his cock seeming to make each orgasm set off another until she screamed with pleasure, arching her back for what seemed like an hour and feeling like a toy that Mike had carelessly broken while playing with it.

At last she fell back against the gray comforter atop Mike's big daddy bed. Mike gathered her up off the bed with one arm around her back and the other under her bottom, his softening cock still inside, and held her in the air, suspended against him, for a few moments. Darla

didn't think she had ever felt anything so wonderful—except maybe his hands on her, seizing her as his own, just before he had come.

The feeling, to her surprise and her shame, once again awakened the need to be naughty, once again set her pussy melting.

"Daddy?" she asked timidly.

"Yes, sweetheart?"

"Am I still going to have a special lesson tonight at bedtime? Even though I had my reward here in your bed?" As she spoke, she realized she didn't know whether she did or didn't want to learn about special lessons tonight.

"Yes, sweetheart. Daddy has to follow through on what he says. Even though what we just did was very special, a special lesson is a way for daddy to make sure you understand your responsibilities. We had some trouble about your toileting, didn't we?"

"Yes, but…" Darla's heart quailed, and now she definitely didn't want a special lesson, even though it made her pussy clench, as Mike carried her around the bed and laid her gently down.

"No buts, Darla. Did we have trouble about your toileting or not?" He sat on the side of the bed, looking down at her where she lay curled up on her side.

"Yes, daddy." She tried to give a brave little smile.

"You've been very good today, but it's important that we continue to build on that compliance, now that it's coming out. You'll have a special lesson." Mike reached down and took her bottom in his big hand. He gave a little squeeze, and Darla whimpered. "You've probably figured out that special lessons involve your backside, haven't you?"

"What are they?" she squeaked. "What are you going to do to my bottom, daddy?"

"You'll find out after dinner tonight, sweetheart," was all he would say. "Now you can stay here in my bed for a few minutes, but then please get into your big-girl panties

and your pinafore and come help with dinner, okay?"

"Okay, daddy." His hand left her bottom, but it still seemed to tingle. Darla found herself wriggling it a little, as if that might tell her something about what awaited her later that evening, but all she felt was more anxiety about what her little rump must undergo. He had told her that now that they were having sex, she must be ready to have her daddy's cock inside her there, in that most shameful way, but she couldn't tell if that necessity of serving her daddy with her anus had anything to do with the special lessons that naughty girls must receive.

All through dinner she could hardly eat any of the delicious chicken Mike had made, and she fidgeted so much that he finally said, "Darla, I promise that I won't make this first special lesson too hard on you. You'd better get ready for it though, right now, so we can get it over with. I'll do the dishes. Take off all your clothes and kneel on your bed and present your bottom the same way you did yesterday when I spanked you there for saying a bad word."

"Yes, daddy," Darla said meekly and rose to obey, feeling a strange sense of relief that despite the humiliating position into which she must get, she would soon know what a special lesson was.

On her bed she waited in that position, thinking about what it meant that she had a daddy who could tell her to present her bottom that way. He had put his cock in her mouth, and in her pussy, and soon—whether it had anything to do with the special lesson or not—she felt sure he would tell her the time had come to put it in her bottom as well. Darla would never have thought she might feel her heart flutter not in fear but in expectation at that thought, and the mental picture that accompanied it, of Mike walking in, naked, cock in hand, to present his hardness to the tiny place where he wanted to claim her as his own naughty little girl.

She heard his step behind her. "Hi, daddy," she said,

trying to crane her neck around to see him.

"Hi, sweetheart," Mike said. "Keep your eyes forward, please. The most important thing about a special lesson is that when a naughty girl has one, she surrenders her bottom to her daddy, for training."

"Training, daddy?" Darla whispered.

"Yes, Darla. Training. Selecta has developed this program around the idea that certain girls can't be obedient and good unless they learn to provide a man's cock with pleasure, when he has anal intercourse with her."

"What?" she gasped. But she realized that she hadn't questioned what her daddy had said, really. In fact, though she couldn't understand why, the idea struck her as somehow to make sense, despite its apparent outlandishness.

"If we hadn't started to have sex, I would have begun to train your bottom only for the right man, who will someday take you in hand and have your bottom when he likes, whether to keep you in line or merely for his daily enjoyment. As it is, though, today daddy will start training you for his own cock, and he'll fuck your bottom tonight to start breaking it in, after your first lesson."

"Oh, God, daddy. Please… not tonight? Tomorrow, maybe?" She spoke to the comforter without knowing whether she meant the words, but so terribly poised between fear and desire that she didn't know what else to do besides ask for a delay in her sentence.

"Who gets to say, Darla?" Mike said sternly.

"Daddy," she answered.

"Then don't try to get out of it, or your special lesson will be a hard one, even though it's your first." He laid his hand on her naked bottom. "Make up your mind that you're going to please your daddy with your bottom tonight, and everything will be easier for you."

"Yes, daddy." She bit her lip, feeling like she might cry any moment, but not really knowing why because, yes,

now that Mike had said that he *would* have her anus tonight, no ifs, ands, or buts, it had seemed to grow the desire and lessen the fear.

The hand left her backside. "Alright," came Mike's voice from behind and above her. "A special lesson starts with cleaning out your anus. I'm going to give you an enema now, sweetheart."

# CHAPTER FOURTEEN

Mike had already lubed the red plastic nozzle he held in his right hand. In his left he had the white silicone bag, full of warm soapy water. He didn't delay, wanting neither to make Darla wait for her enema nor to postpone his pleasure in the cute, naughty, cock-stiffening sight of his little girl with the nozzle up her sweet little bottom.

He put the well-lubed tip right there, right on the crinkly little aperture where he had made her put her finger before, when she had had her orgasmic reward lying on his bed. He pushed gently, but Darla's virginal bottom-hole resisted, her buttocks tightening as if at the thought of having to have something inside her there that her daddy had decided should be in her most private place.

"I know it's difficult, Darla," Mike said, "but soon you're going to have to open up for something much bigger. This is what your special lessons are all about. Little girls have to learn to take what their daddies, and then one day their husbands, give them, even when it's embarrassing and uncomfortable."

"But why?" Darla wailed. "Daddy, it feels so funny! Why do I have to have an enema?"

Mike didn't respond with words, at first, but instead

simply pushed the nozzle in, overcoming Darla's resistance and making her cry out in shame as she felt her anus stretched around the plastic. Her bottom continued to clench, trying to push the thing out, but Mike held it tightly in, trying to demonstrate as clearly as possible to her that her bottom must accept his discipline in whatever form he meted it out for her improvement.

"Daddy!" Darla cried, her head rearing back and then bowing down again to the comforter between her forearms. He could tell she had her boo-boo face on.

"You need to have regular enemas while you're in this program, sweetheart, because nothing will make you as conscious of the need not just for hygiene and bodily cleanliness, but also for cleansing on the inside. When I open the valve and the soapy water starts to flow into your rear end, I want you to think about what kind of a girl you want to be. Do you want to be the kind of girl who needs to have an enema to teach her a lesson, who has to be put into diapers because she can't obey her daddy, who has to have a trip across her daddy or her husband's knee every day? Or do you want to be the kind of girl who wears grownup clothes and gets to make choices, because she understands that her daddy and her husband know what's best for her, and she obeys them?"

Mike laid the bag on her naked back for a moment so he could shift his left hand to her pert bottom and hold the nozzle in with that hand, while with his right he turned the little valve on the hose, then picked up the bag.

"Oh!" Darla said, as the rushing sound of the warm water sounded faintly in the air. "Oh, daddy…" Again her head went back, and again she bowed it.

"Which kind of girl do you want to be?" Mike asked softly.

Darla gave a little sob. Then she whispered, "I want to be a good girl, daddy."

"You're learning very well, sweetheart," Mike said, using his fingers around the nozzle to caress her sweet

bottom-cheeks a little. "Having daddy's cock in here later will be a very important moment for you, won't it?"

"Yes, daddy."

Mike gave the enema bag a gentle squeeze to propel more water into his little girl's bottom. Darla moaned.

"You'll be nice and clean, won't you, sweetheart? You won't get your trainer or daddy's cock dirty."

"M-my… t-trainer?"

"That's what comes after you've gone to the potty and washed up, Darla. I'll use the small trainer tonight, but we need to start opening you, and the program requires that by the time you graduate you'll be wearing a nice, thick one once a week for at least three hours." He gave the bag another squeeze: Darla had taken almost the whole pint, now.

"Oh, no," she whispered. "Please, daddy?"

"Selecta says so, Darla, and I would train you this way even if it weren't a required part of the program. You need this kind of lesson very much. Once you're done with this first lesson tonight, and I've put my seed in your bottom, I think you'll understand much better how important it is for a girl like you to know her backside belongs to a man who knows how to guide her and how to protect her." The water had all flowed out of the bag, and Darla had begun to make uncomfortable little noises as every small movement of her legs caused it to slosh inside her rear end. "Do you think you're starting to understand?"

"Yes, daddy," Darla said meekly to her comforter. "It's so embarrassing, though!"

"I know, sweetheart. It's meant to be, to make you think about your behavior and your choices. I'm going to pull the nozzle out, now, and go put it away. You'll stay here for ten minutes with the soapy water inside you and your bottom still well presented, and then you'll be allowed to go to the potty. After that you'll take a shower, and then you'll report to my den, and get yourself over the special stool I've put there. Then I'll train your bottom with your

first trainer."

"Will it hurt, daddy?" The sweetness of her voice seemed to speak of a new pleasure she had begun to find in submitting to her daddy's instructions.

"Yes, Darla, I'm afraid it will, especially this first time. But I promise that if you're a good girl and you learn to accept your training obediently and respectfully, you'll begin to enjoy it, too—maybe even tonight, at least a little bit. Naughty little girls learn to love anal training, because they know their daddies like to see a cute bottom nice and full of whatever daddy wants to put there, and they know how hard it gets their daddies to train them that way."

In Mike's den the special stool, provided by Selecta, waited in the middle of the carpet. On an end table waited the pink butt-plug and the lube. Selecta had sent a box of five plugs, all in different shades of pink, from this pale pink length of hard rubber, as long as Mike's index finger and not much thicker, to the hot pink one as long as his whole hand and as wide, at its widest point—just above the indentation that would secure it inside Darla's rectum—as three of his fingers.

*You will quickly gain a sense of your naughty little girl's needs in this area, and enforce special lessons accordingly,* ran the program manual. *In general, the No. 3 plug serves as the best baseline: it fulfills the graduation requirement and has sufficient length and thickness to make it clear to most girls that their anuses have been well attended to, and that they must expect to be trained there by their eventual husbands.*

*The Nos. 4 and 5 plugs should in most cases be reserved for severer discipline, unless a sexual relationship has developed between you and your naughty little girl. In that case, you will find that the No. 4 gets your girl ready for the deep anal penetration you will wish to demand of her, and you should step her up to it quickly so that you need not delay your pleasures. You will want to enjoy her there even before you've widened her, of course, and such is to be sure your right, once this part of your custody of your naughty little girl has come into*

*its own.*

*Selecta strongly advises, though, that you break in her anus gently in those early days, as it will produce much better results as her training continues. Your naughty little girl shouldn't fear anal sex as much as she understands that it is something she must undergo despite the discomfort and shame associated, because you are in charge of her anus, just as you are in charge of the rest of her.*

*If you do have anal sex with your naughty little girl, and use the No. 4 plug as a regular training device to make your pleasure in her backside greater, the No. 5 plug will then be your disciplinary solution, should she require something severe. On the other hand, the benefits of correcting her with your penis itself, in a truly rigorous session of anal intercourse (see also our training video 'When a girl needs a butt-fucking'), should never be overlooked. The plug and daddy's penis are not mutually exclusive as disciplinary instruments, of course; you may very well wish to use them in tandem.*

The special stool, made of shiny chrome, rose three feet off the floor. It had been sized to Darla's measurements, and had a padded top, upholstered in pink, that would go under her hips when she bent over it to receive what her daddy decided to give her. It had a bar at its base for her to hold onto while she had her special lesson.

When Darla entered the room, Mike was sitting in his easy chair—the same chair he had sat in, of course, when Darla gave him her first blowjob only the previous night. It seemed like weeks ago now. When he saw her quail back a little at the sight of the stool and the plug and turn pink, Mike realized that in a matter of not much more than two days, he had developed an affection for this spirited but fundamentally pure-hearted eighteen-year-old. The thought that ultimately he must train her for another man—the 'right' man—to come along bothered him a little, then, for the first time.

"All clean, sweetheart?" he asked his naked little girl as she seemed to hover in the doorway to his sanctum.

"All clean, daddy," she said. Her face turned scarlet. "It was a little messy."

"I know, sweetheart," Mike said indulgently. "That's just the way it is. Sometimes we have to be messy to get clean. Now your bottom is nice and clean for training, and for daddy to fuck it." He watched the crease deepen between her cute brunette eyebrows with great satisfaction. She had compressed her lips into a tight line and she seemed rooted to the spot, with her right hand covering her pussy and her left hand behind, covering her bottom in what looked like a charming, cock-stiffening instinctive gesture, as if to protect her most private places from the lesson she knew was coming to them.

"Go ahead and get over your training stool, Darla," he said, making his voice a little more stern. "That's enough dawdling. And take your hands away from your privates and put them on your head. You know better than to try to hide your pussy and your bottom from your daddy."

Darla gave a little gasp of which even she seemed unable fully to grasp the nature. "Please, daddy," she whispered, her hands moving slowly and uncertainly to obey him. "Please be gentle with me."

"Daddy knows your bottom has never had a cock inside it, sweetheart," Mike said. "That's why we're going to start with the little plug, and with only the tip of daddy's cock tonight. Daddy will finish between your little bottom-cheeks and not inside your little flower."

"Oh," Darla said, as if she had never thought of all the different possibilities—the various things that a knowledgeable daddy might do with her young bottom.

"If you want daddy to be gentle, though, you need to get yourself over the stool, and show me that you know how to follow my instructions, even when it means getting ready for a special lesson in your bottom."

# CHAPTER FIFTEEN

Darla didn't know how she could manage to put her hands on her head for the short trip to the stool in the middle of the carpet, let alone lay herself over that stool with its pink padded top. It wouldn't really be terribly uncomfortable, she could see, just truly humiliating—at least before the main part of the lesson began. But ever since she had seen the video Selecta had made her watch, of Frannie about to have a special lesson, she had somehow known it must be something like this, and she had also known that she couldn't, just couldn't, submit to it.

She looked at Mike, though, and suddenly she realized that she *could* do it, because if she didn't do it she knew her daddy would spank her, or even whip her. He had the look on his face that Darla had learned meant that he was being patient with his little girl now, but that in just a moment he would decide that she needed firmer guidance than he had given her yet, and that he once again needed to demonstrate that being a good girl meant respecting his instructions.

She moved her hands up, watching them tremble as they rose into the air in front of her, leaving behind the

places that she just instinctively felt the need to hide even though she did know that part of her program with her daddy demanded that he got to see her naked—*all* of her naked—including nipples and pussy and bottom, the parts that even though it seemed so wicked, daddies liked to see and had a right to see.

To know that Mike would spank her if she failed to obey seemed not to make her afraid, the way Darla supposed she might have felt about it, had she tried to imagine three days ago what it might be like to have a big, strong, older man in charge of her—a man who had the authority, and even the obligation, to discipline her with his big hand and with his stout belt, on her bare little bottom. Instead, though she certainly still didn't *want* to be spanked (even if she had been so desperate to know what the belt felt like, earlier that evening when her daddy had been about to fuck her), she felt like knowing that her daddy wouldn't hesitate to give her the correction she needed just made things easier, as if where before she had to ponder and overthink everything, now she only had to follow her daddy's rules and obey his instructions.

She looked at the stool, and in her imagination she saw herself lying over it with her little bottom the highest part of her, gripping the bar and spreading her legs to give her daddy access to the tiny hole where she must have her lesson. She felt her face flush hotly at the mental picture, but then next to it she saw Mike coming for her and dragging her over his lap in his big easy chair, and spanking her harder and harder until she cried out that she would have her special lesson; she would get over the nasty stool and have the shameful pink trainer put in her bottom.

Darla looked into Mike's face, and saw the spanking coming. "Last chance, sweetheart," he said, with a note of warning in his voice.

She took a step forward, and then another. Two more and she would be in front of the stool. Her hands had

reached the top of her head while she had been thinking about how humiliating a posture she must now take, so that she hadn't even noticed the embarrassment of exposing herself that way to her daddy.

Another step. She looked at the stool, then back at Mike, still sitting in his big chair. She felt her brow pucker. "Daddy?" she asked.

She saw impatience cross his handsome face, but then he seemed to sense that Darla needed a softer sort of response.

"Yes, sweetheart?"

"Do you think I'm pretty?" Darla wasn't sure why she felt she needed to know the answer to that question so very badly right now, but something in her cried out for the reassurance that her daddy liked to see her naked. Somehow she thought it might make it easier to go over the stool.

A puzzled expression appeared on Mike's face. He seemed for a moment to be trying to figure out whether to take the question seriously and, if so, how to answer it. Then, without saying anything, he got up from his chair and came over to Darla and put his arms around her, which was a little strange because her hands were on top of her head.

"You can hug me, sweetheart," he said, and Darla did, and it felt wonderful to be enclosed in that hug, her daddy with all his clothes on embracing his naked little girl before he taught her the special lesson, reassuring her that everything would be just fine.

"I think you're the prettiest little girl I've ever seen," he said softly right into her ear. His whiskers had grown during the day, of course, and they tickled her cheek and made her giggle a little. "I can't imagine anything more wonderful than having a little girl like you to take care of, and to teach to please me and to give special treats to."

"Thanks, daddy," she whispered back. "I want to be a good girl for you, but it's so embarrassing sometimes."

"I know, Darla," he said. "Do you think you understand why I have to give you special lessons?"

"Yes, daddy."

"Then get your sweet little backside over the stool. It's time. No more dawdling, or you'll feel my hand across that tushy."

He released her from the hug, and turned her around to face the stool. Then, to her startled alarm, he brought his hand down on her bottom once, very sharply, so that the spank rang out like a gunshot.

"Ow!" she cried. She put her hands behind her to try to rub away the sting.

"There's a lot more where that came from, Darla," Mike said. "You know what you need to do."

"Yes, daddy," she said, and finally she began to bend herself over the stool with the pink padded top, running her hands down to support herself as she did, along the cross-trussed chrome bars that made up its sturdy legs.

It wasn't uncomfortable, but it was very awkward. As she felt her daddy putting his hands inside her knees to pull them firmly apart so that they were on either side of the frame that supported the stool, the humiliation of having to adopt that posture, with her backside so high and so open and her head hanging down, sent the blood rushing to her face even more than the position would have by itself.

If her daddy wanted to, he could just put his cock inside her pussy, Darla thought wantonly, unable to help the images that passed through her mind as in her imagination she pictured what she must look like. He could just enter his little girl and ride her as long as he wanted. He could keep her over the stool for hours and hours and put his big hard cock in her when he felt like it.

Or he could spank her with his hand, or whip her with his belt. If he wanted. Then he might put his cock in again and enjoy himself for a few minutes. Daddy got to say, and his little girl had to stay over the stool with her pussy and

her bottom ready for daddy to use whatever way he liked best.

Or… he could put his big, hard cock somewhere else. Somewhere no one had ever put anything besides a thermometer, when Darla was very small, until her daddy had cleaned her out with the terrible enema a few minutes before.

His voice came from behind her and what seemed far, far above her. "It's time for your special lesson, Darla," she heard him say. "I'm going to put the No. 1 trainer inside your bottom now. Even though it's little, it's shaped so that you won't be able to push it out. Do you understand what that means?"

Darla felt her upper lip quiver. "What does it mean, daddy?"

"It means that when I put something in your bottom, it will stay there as long as I decide it should. Special lessons are a way to teach you that your bottom belongs to your daddy until he's sure you've become a good girl. Then, later, your bottom will belong to your husband, because that's what girls like you need—a firm hand and a stiff cock, applied to your most intimate place."

Darla couldn't understand why something deep, deep inside her seemed to agree with what Mike had said, despite its being so wrong from the perspective of everything she had thought she learned, growing up in modern society. She said, hardly hesitating at all, "Yes, daddy." It didn't make the prospect of having the thing inside her little bottom-hole any more attractive or less shameful, but somehow knowing that her daddy knew exactly what she needed made her feel better about, well, everything.

She heard a snapping sound, and she knew it must be her daddy opening the little bottle of lube she had seen on the end table. Then a little silence, and Darla knew her daddy was putting the lube on the pink training plug that would go into her tiny flower. She realized again then just

how open she lay, over the stool; daddy wouldn't even have to spread her cheeks, or tell Darla to spread them— no, daddy must just be looking right at the crinkly button in the narrow furrow of his little girl's young bottom, getting ready to put the trainer inside it.

The trainer that would train *her*… train her to receive a man's penis where a penis wasn't supposed to go, unless a girl happened to be the kind of girl who needed such shameful things. Daddy had fucked her, but that wasn't enough, Darla knew. Not nearly enough. Daddy must fuck her in the most wicked, naughty way, to teach her to be good.

It touched her; the cool, slippery tip of the plug touched her little flower. Darla gave a whimpering cry at the feeling—the way the narrowness began to push in, becoming wider, opening her, making her little ring burn and itch. Her bottom clenched instinctively.

"Oh, no… please, daddy, no," she moaned. "Not yet. I'm so little back there."

"Don't be silly, Darla," Mike said sternly. "Your bottom was made to open much wider than this. You just need to learn how to accept it, when daddy puts something here. Relax your bottom, the way you do on the potty, and daddy will put the trainer inside you."

But Darla couldn't. Instead, her bottom-cheeks surged, trying to close though because of the way Mike had positioned her over the stool she knew they couldn't tighten enough to conceal the aperture where he continued to press the tip of the trainer.

"I'm sorry, daddy," she wailed. "I want to be a good girl!"

"Good girls open their bottoms, sweetheart," Mike said, and then he pushed very, very firmly.

Darla heard a whining cry of alarm and discomfort come from her chest, but her daddy kept pushing the thing inside. She cried out again, and then she realized that Mike had forced the trainer inside, and now she had it inside her

bottom even though she hadn't accepted it.

Mike began to pull and push on the plug, and Darla moaned each time she felt it move inside and open her little flower again, from the other direction.

"This is the most important part of the lesson," her daddy said. "I'm teaching you to open more fully next time. We'll do this for a few minutes. I want you to think about having a man take his pleasure inside your bottom. As I said, daddy won't do more than put the head of his cock inside tonight, but it won't be long before he rides your little bottom with his penis all the way inside, and puts his seed inside you when he's done."

# CHAPTER SIXTEEN

Darla sobbed now, as Mike drew the little plug almost all the way out, then seated it back inside her, then did it again. He said nothing as he trained her anus, letting his manipulations of the plug teach her at a level deeper than words could. He repeated that part of the lesson five times.

After that, with some difficulty because Darla still hadn't learned how to open her anus, he pulled the plug all the way out, supplying all the necessary force himself. Then, immediately, Mike forced the narrow pink trainer back in, as Darla cried out in discomfort at the rigors of having a special lesson from her daddy.

Mike couldn't get over how distractingly adorable his little girl looked over the stool with the little pink plug peeping saucily out between her spread cheeks. He left the plug where it was for a few moments, and began to stroke her wonderful pert bottom-cheeks very gently, as her little whimpers continued.

"It's time to learn how to be a good girl, Darla," he said, breaking the near-silence. "In a moment I'm going to pull on the plug, and you're going to show me how you can open, to help me pull it out. Then it will be time for

daddy to put his penis inside."

Another little sob. Then, "Yes, daddy," in a small voice. "I'll try. I want my bottom to belong to you."

"That's all I can ask, sweetheart," Mike said, and tugged gently on the base of the plug.

Darla whimpered, and then to Mike's satisfaction her little bottom-cheeks surged outward as she at last learned to do what she must. The pink plug emerged, pushed out from her tight young anus by Mike's naughty little girl, who gave a cry of shame as if at the discovery that she must do something that felt so terribly dirty to show herself obedient to her daddy.

Mike helped the plug along only a little bit, and then he pulled it entirely free of Darla's bottom. "There we go," he said. "That wasn't so hard, was it?"

"No, daddy," she said sweetly.

Mike put the plug back on the end table. "You'll wash the plug after I'm through with you, sweetheart," he said. "Even though you're nice and clean in there from your enema, hygiene is still very important, and girls like you, who need a lot of anal training, have to learn to keep their trainers clean. For now, though, daddy's cock is very hard and he needs to be inside his little girl right away."

Whimpery moans were Darla's only response as he quickly dropped his jeans and briefs, then stripped his T-shirt off, marveling at how hard his cock had gotten as he trained his little girl's bottom for her own good, and for his pleasure. Not for the first time, Mike wondered whether he himself might be the right man for her; certainly he didn't mind giving it a serious attempt.

*Approximately 43% of correctional officers develop a sexual relationship with their naughty little girls,* the Selecta manual read. *As long as the officer is careful to maintain proper discipline in his house, and to dominate his naughty little girl in their consensual sexual activities, the benefits for her rehabilitation can be great, while no negative effects have been observed.*

*Of the sexual relationships that develop between correctional officers and naughty little girls, approximately 63% mature into long-term commitments; 82% of these long-term couples eventually marry. Though the relative newness of the Daddy's Naughty Little Girl program (these data were observed in the pilot program in New Jersey) prevents a truly longitudinal dataset at this point, these relationships between daddies and their naughty little girls give every sign of being lifelong commitments that might well prove highly beneficial to the social fabric of our communities.*

*To that end, if a sexual relationship does develop between you and your little girl, it is extremely important that you make it as clear as you can to her that she is the subservient sexual partner. The girls chosen for the program need this more than any other single facet of the relationship, though the sense that you will take care of her and make sure nothing harms her runs a very close second.*

*Thus, you must be careful to have sex with your naughty little girl dominantly, the way she needs it. When you give her an ordinary special lesson with the trainer you have chosen for her anus that day, you do not ask her permission or her opinion on whether she should have to have a plug in her rectum, or how big that plug should be.*

*If a sexual relationship has developed, in just the same way, when you augment a special lesson by the imposition of your penis in any of her pleasurable orifices or in some other way, such as between her breasts or between her buttocks, you must make certain to give your naughty little girl the strongest possible impression that she is having sex because her daddy has decided the time has come for her to have sex. When you have sex with her outside of disciplinary activity, similarly, for example if you decide to visit her room in the night and enjoy her there, or you bring her to daddy's bed for 'big-girl time,' you should try to ensure that she understands that she will have to receive her daddy's penis wherever he wants to put it in her body, and for as long as he chooses to enjoy her.*

Mike touched the head of his cock to his little girl's well-lubed flower. "Be brave, sweetheart," he said softly.

"Okay, daddy," she whispered back.

Holding his cock steady in his left hand, and stroking

Darla's bottom gently with his right, he leaned forward, pushing firmly. Darla cried out, and then, to Mike's gratified surprise, her bottom gave the little surge she had just learned, and received the penis inside it.

"Oh, God," Darla moaned. "Oh, daddy, it's too big! It's too big!"

"Hush, sweetheart. It's not too big. You have it inside you now. Daddy's just going to have a tiny little fuck in your bottom now."

Mike loved anal sex. Something about the way it felt wrong to make a girl do that, to make her take a hard cock up her cute little butt, seemed at the same time to make it also feel so very right, if you had the right girl in your bed—or, he supposed, over the special stool your employer sent for the purpose. He had had the asses of three girls before, and he was proud to say that he had broken in each one of those asses so well that the girls, despite their initial fears, had all ended up loving to hear Mike say that he would fuck her in the tushy that night.

He had never been as ready to sheathe his hard cock deep in an ass as he was now, to fuck Darla there long and hard. With his little girl positioned so perfectly over the stool, with her bottom spread and her butthole relaxed from the plug, he knew he could easily go back on his word and ride her adorable rump without compunction, holding her hips firmly, until he had shot his seed deep in her bowels. She would cry out at the indignity, and at his little betrayal, but she would also feel proud of herself for having endured the shameful ordeal of her daddy's big cock at full length up her backside, and she would have the very important experience of feeling her daddy's semen trickling out of her, reminding her that her bottom now belonged to him.

But not only did the Selecta manual emphasize consistency and promise-keeping, but Mike himself knew that he could not be such a monstrous caricature of a caring daddy to his little girl. He had promised to break her

helps. But…"

"But what?" Mike asked curiously, still stroking the cute lips so that Darla's arousal would flow, and she would go to bed wishing she were allowed to play with herself.

"But will you put your cock in my little pussy again soon, daddy?" she blurted out.

Mike chuckled and took his hand away, then patted her bottom. "Daddy will have you both ways from now on, sweetheart. Don't worry. Daddy's going to wake you up nice and early tomorrow, and have you lie on your tummy in your bed, so he can get into your pussy from behind, and give you a good-morning fuck like that, lying on top of you. Will you like that?"

"Yes, daddy," Darla whispered.

# CHAPTER SEVENTEEN

The next few weeks, and then months, went by in a blur of morning big-girl time and evening big-girl time, and special lessons at least once a week. At work, Joanne seemed to say every day how much happier Darla looked than she ever had before. At first, Darla didn't like to admit that it had taken the Daddy's Naughty Little Girl program to teach her how to live her life, but then to her surprise she got promoted to parts manager—over Joanne's head, though Joanne didn't seem angry about it.

"You deserve it, honey," Joanne said. "You've been working your butt off."

Darla blushed despite the clear lack of intended double-meaning in Joanne's words. Joanne seemed to notice the blush, and she giggled.

"Don't try to pretend that it's not because of your *daddy*," she said, dropping her voice to a conspiratorial whisper for the final word.

Darla felt her mouth twist to her side, but then she giggled. "I won't. Daddy's going to be so proud of me!"

Mike did indeed make much of her that night, and treated her like a little princess. He wouldn't let her help with dinner or even do the dishes, but instead he made her

favorite dinner, spaghetti and meatballs with no green stuff in the meatballs, and let her pick a movie to watch. Something about being Mike's little girl in a disciplinary sense had regressed her tastes, too; she still liked grownup movies and foods and things, but she had rediscovered the sheer joy of childhood as well, and she didn't even mind wearing her pinafore in the evening, and her little-girl nightgown in bed—when her daddy let her wear clothes, that is.

She chose a fairy princess movie, and Mike held her in his lap in his big chair as they watched it. He had had her change into her nightgown, with no panties, before they started the movie, but he didn't seem to have any plans to have big-girl time with her in the near future. He just held her tight and stroked her hair from time to time.

Darla liked that just fine for the first half of the movie, but about two-thirds of the way through, when the fairies had gone off on some quest for a magic necklace, she found that she had started to fidget.

"Stop squirming, Darla," Mike said. He didn't speak sharply, but, as always, his voice had an essential firmness that seemed to send a sort of lightning bolt of arousal through Darla's body.

"I'll try, daddy," she whispered. Then she attempted to pay attention to the blue fairy's impassioned speech about friendship, but instead she kept thinking that daddy's lap felt a little like his penis might be getting hard. Had she done that with her squirming?

Something made her squirm again, even though *most* of her didn't mean to. Was daddy's penis hard, or wasn't it? Suddenly she felt desperate to know.

"Sweetheart, what's gotten into you?" Mike asked, in a voice that mingled surprise and annoyance. "Do you not like the movie?"

"I like it fine, daddy," Darla said, and now she heard a note of sass in her voice that she hadn't expected. What was going on?

"Well, your tone of voice doesn't seem to match up with your words, young lady. Watch your attitude, please." He still seemed to be keeping his patience, but Darla thought she could tell he wouldn't keep it for much longer.

"I said I like it fine. I don't see why I have to watch my attitude."

"Darla," Mike said sharply. "I can see that you don't care for the movie after all. Why don't you go to your room and get ready for bed?"

He lifted her off his lap and set her on her feet. She turned to face him, highly dissatisfied with the situation, which now seemed to have gone in the wrong direction, though Darla couldn't have said what the right direction might be.

"No, I'm not going to bed. I got promoted today. I'm going to watch some real TV."

"Young lady," Mike said, his voice now very stern. "I'm sorry tonight turned out this way. I'm very proud of you for your promotion, but you're still in my custody. If you had approached this differently, you could certainly have watched big-girl TV, but you're showing that you need me to set a serious boundary here."

Then he spoke so solemnly that the words made Darla's heart pound in her chest. "You only have two weeks left of the program, and I have to be able to tell the board that you're ready to leave my custody, or you're going to be here for another six months. I can't graduate you unless I'm sure I've taught you everything I can about keeping a proper attitude toward authority. I have to punish you severely. You'll have a belt-whipping and a special lesson for your behavior tonight. Go get ready for the enema; I want your butt nice and high so I can whip it before I clean it out."

"What?!" Darla's stomach had started doing flip-flops the moment Mike had reminded her that the program had nearly finished, but the news of the special lesson now made her shake like a leaf. But she saw in Mike's face his

complete seriousness, and she understood in a flash of insight that he had figured out instinctually exactly what she needed, and exactly what she had been doing: subconsciously, Darla craved the kind of discipline only a special lesson could give. The only question was whether she could bear to receive it, for her daddy clearly intended to make sure she understood he was ready to give her as much of it as he thought she deserved, and she deserved a lot.

"Please, daddy, not the No. 5?" Darla wailed.

She had had the No. 4 in her little flower weekly for the past month, and her daddy had praised how open her bottom was getting. He loved to tell her how nice it made his cock feel to push it in all the way even though Darla still cried out in discomfort when he made her have the whole thing in her anus. When he used her roughly there, too, as he had once or twice, as if overcome with the pleasure her tight little bottom provided, she would be very sore the next day, but the way Mike cuddled her in bed after he fucked her over the stool always seemed to make even that soreness feel good, somehow.

"Yes, the No. 5, Darla. I need to make sure you learn your lesson. You'll have the No. 5 for ten minutes, and then daddy will fuck your butt and put his seed there."

Darla felt herself starting to cry, but she realized to her surprise that the tears weren't really fearful. She whispered, "And if I'm a good girl for my whipping and my special lesson?"

Suddenly a smile broke out on Mike's face, to Darla's surprised relief. "If you're a good girl, you'll get a reward, sweetheart. Especially since it's your big day."

"Thanks, daddy," she said softly. "I'll go get ready for my punishment."

As she took off her nightgown, she wondered whether she would ever be able to figure out how the discipline, the sex, and the return to childhood related to one another, or whether it simply went beyond what the human mind

could grasp. She folded the nightgown and put it atop her dresser. She climbed onto her little-girl bed, in which she now slept so very soundly and securely, with the knowledge that she might wake up to find her daddy's penis at her lips and have to swallow his seed before she rose to take her morning shower, or might find herself being carried to her daddy's bed and laid on her tummy for him to slip into her bare pussy and ride her until he came inside, after she had had little climax after little climax all through, because of how skillfully he always played with her clit while he fucked.

If she graduated, would it ever be the same? Would her daddy still discipline her? Would he still treat her like his favorite sex-toy, the way Darla had blushingly come to love, telling her that it was big-girl time and she must receive his cock the way a big girl does when she knows her place and her duties?

Was *that* why she had acted up that way?

She arched her back, even though it made her blush. She wanted daddy to see his favorite bare bottom waiting obediently for him to punish, clean out, and prepare for his pleasure. She wanted daddy to know that when he finally put his penis inside her, his naughty little girl understood what it meant—that Darla belonged to her daddy, Mike, and didn't want to stop belonging to him.

"I have to whip you now, sweetheart," Mike said from behind her.

"Yes, daddy," Darla said. She felt his left hand come down upon her waist and then the whipping started, hard and quick. Even though a moment before she had wanted so badly to show that she could receive her punishment like a big girl, the pain from her daddy's thick leather belt was so great that she tried to crawl up the bed and escape, crying out, "Please, not so hard, daddy!"

But Mike, as usual, held her tightly around the waist, then, and kept whipping her. "Think about how your backside feels right now, the next time you're deciding

how to behave, Darla. Your butt is getting whipped for your own good, to help you learn."

Darla had started to sob. "I'm sorry, daddy. I'll be good." Her bottom felt like Mike's belt had caught fire and was burning her in bright lines of pain.

"I know you will," Mike said then, stopping the whipping. For a few brief moments, he rubbed her bottom as Darla sighed, but then he said, "Time for your enema, sweetheart. Because you were naughty, you'll have another pint tonight."

He had brought the terrible bag, with its hose and its nozzle. Darla had had an enema every week since she came to her daddy's house, but she didn't think she could ever get used to it. Now the news that she would have twice as much of the warm soapy water up her bottom made her boo-boo face come out. "I can't, daddy! I won't make it to the bathroom!"

"Yes, you will. It won't be fun, but the way you behaved, fun isn't something I'm trying to provide." He stuck the nozzle into Darla's punished bottom and she felt her cheeks go scarlet the way they always did when the warm water started to flow the wrong way and she pictured the way her bottom looked to Mike as he prepared it to receive what he would give it over the stool.

"There you go," Mike said, pulling the nozzle out.

As she waited to be allowed to go to the bathroom, she seemed to give a continual whine at the terrible fullness. Did she really want this to continue past the next two weeks? Was this what she wanted? Was she crazy?

"Alright," Mike said after what seemed like only five minutes. "You can go to the potty, sweetheart. Then, have a quick shower and come get over your stool for your tushy-training."

To take her mind off the horrible embarrassment of voiding the enema—the shameful sounds and the shamefully arousing feelings—Darla thought about the thrill of arousal that had gone through her at the way Mike

had called the special lesson *tushy-training*. No, she would never fully understand it, but something about the way the childish word *tushy* made her feel when her daddy associated it with *training*, and the way that idea conveyed how he wanted Darla to be his special girl, the girl whose bottom he trained up for himself... well, maybe she *was* crazy, but that didn't change the fact that Mike made her feel safe and loved when he informed her that the time had come for her tushy-training.

"Daddy?" she said once she had gone over the stool, in her now-familiar position, and Mike had started, she thought—though of course in her posture she couldn't see it—to lube the big, big plug.

"Yes, sweetheart?" All his sternness seemed to have gone, whether in the satisfaction of the stern lesson he had taught her with his belt or perhaps in the anticipation of the way his cock would feel when he pressed it deep into Darla's trained tushy and rode her there until he had spurted his seed as far inside as his big penis could go.

"What if I didn't graduate? What if I never did? What if I were always your naughty little girl? Would you keep taking care of me? And... you know... punishing me, and things?"

Mike chuckled. She heard him put down the plug, and then he was lifting her up from the stool and carrying her to the big chair. He sat her in his lap again, naked this time, and now she didn't squirm because she knew beyond a shadow of a doubt how very hard she had made her daddy's cock.

"I love you, Darla," he said, looking into her eyes. "If you want, you can graduate from the program as far as Selecta and the courts are concerned, but stay here anyway and be my little girl."

She blushed very hotly as she felt that her daddy had his hand under her bottom, and had started, it seemed, to give her her reward early, running two fingers back and forth in that way Darla imagined only a girl's daddy could

ever really know how to do.

"Yes, daddy," she said softly, burrowing her cheek into his chest with a little sigh of pleasure. "I'd like that. I love you, too."

"You're not getting out of your special lesson," Mike murmured, "but I think you should come for your daddy now."

Darla gave a whimpery little cry at the way her daddy accompanied his words with a firm circle around her tiny clit. "Daddy gets to say," she said in a voice that was half moan.

"Yes," Mike confirmed. "Daddy gets to say."

# THE END

33926571R00071

Made in the USA
San Bernardino, CA
27 April 2019